This book should be returned to any branch of the Lancashire County Library on or before the date shown

Lancashire County Library
Bowran Street
Preston PR1 2UX

Lancashire
County Council

www.lancashire.gov.uk/libraries

SPANISH RANGE

LEE E. WELLS

S SAGEBRUSH
Large Print Westerns

First published in Great Britain by ISIS Publishing
First published in the United States by Rinehart

Published in Large Print 2011 by ISIS Publishing Ltd.,
7 Centremead, Osney Mead, Oxford OX2 0ES
by arrangement with
Golden West Literary Agency

British Library Cataloguing in Publication Data
Wells, Lee E., 1907–1982.
 Spanish range.
 1. Western stories.
 2. Large type books.
 I. Title
 813.5'4–dc22   11734505

ISBN 978–0–7531–8748–7 (pb)

Printed and bound in Great Britain by
T. J. International Ltd., Padstow, Cornwall

CHAPTER
ONE

It was the last stage of the long journey, and the most crowded. There were four passengers besides Blaise Randell and his partner in the stagecoach, each of them sitting stiff and aloof from his neighbor. Blaise sat next to the window, facing the rear. His long legs cramped back against the seat in his care not to annoy the girl opposite him.

The man beside her cast sidelong glances, but she studiously kept her face toward the window, slender shoulders prim, hands folded over a large purse. The man leaned forward, clearing his throat, forcing her attention. He was portly, with a round, flushed face and watery, salacious eyes. He smiled and touched his pearl-gray derby.

"I hope I ain't disturbing you, ma'am."

She looked coldly at him then turned back to the window, speaking over her shoulder in a clear, musical voice. "Not at all."

"Glad to know it, ma'am." He sank back. He caught Blaise's level look and his eyebrows arched as his lips made a silent whistle. Blaise simply looked and the man flushed, eyes sliding away.

Blaise gave his attention to the world that wheeled by the narrow stagecoach window. The last straggling house of Los Angeles slid by, a little dim in the dust kicked up by the churning hoofs and rolling wheels. Even that town had changed in the time he'd been gone. Everything had changed . . . not in big, important ways, but the little things that a man knew and understood. Los Angeles had grown and he'd heard talk that they were bringing whole trainloads of people out here from the East.

He shifted irritably. This had been range country down here since the days when the Spaniards had shipped out tallow and hides, and mission herds had grazed the San Fernando and San Gabriel valleys. It didn't make sense to clutter it up with Easterners who wouldn't know a riata from a cinch and who would probably farm it anyway.

The coach sped on, paralleling the range of mountains that extended westward from Los Angeles to the sea, the low, rounded hills growing steadily higher. Hal King nudged Blaise, jerking him from his thoughts.

"Pretty country. Is your place like this?"

Blaise smiled, a slow move of the lips as though an unaccustomed action. It lighted his somber, deep-set eyes and strangely softened the angular cheeks and jawbones. For a moment something of the past looked through.

"Almost, only the mountains are closer all around." He nodded toward the window. "But it's all pretty this time of year, right after the spring rains. I'm glad they let . . . I come down right now."

2

Hal nodded. The stage rolled on, the six passengers silent, each in a world of his own. The girl kept her face to the window but she could see the tall young man from the corner of her eyes. He was puzzling. Just now he had smiled and looked almost handsome . . . then his face had settled into deep, harsh lines, as though he had lived with something ugly and hidden.

His voice had sounded slow and deep. He looked like an average ranch worker, except that his cheap clothes were new and somehow a little undersized and uncomfortable, as though he had picked them blindly from a shelf and put them on. Only his boots and gun belt looked right, polished, new, and yet an integral part of him.

Suddenly his eyes swerved to her, alarmed and suspicious. She looked away shocked. She had seen the same expression in the eyes of animals that had suddenly been trapped. Now she knew that there was something wrong about his skin. It should have been a deep tan for he was obviously a man of the outdoors. But it wasn't . . . it was too white.

The man beside her inched closer then leaned around, pointing out the window.

"Now there's one of the biggest old Spanish grants in this part of the country." She gave him a scathing look that he met with a wide grin.

"New here, ain't you? My name's Scarne, Joseph Johnson Scarne, selling the finest line of hardware south of the Techachapis. Ain't nothing —"

"I'm really not interested," she said.

Scarne sank back, eyes round. He chuckled, shrugged and looked at the others. Blaise studied Scarne, steadily, eyes unmoving, hardly blinking. Scarne took it for a while and then he fidgeted, pulled out a cigar, put it back after a quick look at the girl. Blaise still watched, impersonally. Scarne fidgeted a bit more.

"Nice day," he said and Blaise didn't answer. He tried again. "You ain't new to these parts, I take it?"

"No . . . not new."

Scarne nodded, pleased with himself. "I can always tell. You been to Los Angeles, maybe buying supplies or selling beef. You're going back —"

"Where I've been or where I'm going," Blaise said in an even, emotionless voice, "is no business of yours."

Scarne blinked, lost his smile. Then his brashness returned and he nudged the girl. She jumped, startled, and Scarne laughed.

"Now he's —"

"She ain't interested, mister," Blaise said. "Why don't you settle down, or go to sleep?"

A deep flush flowed upward from Scarne's collar. His fat hands clenched and he glared at Blaise. But something in the tall man's steady gaze, the potential power in the relaxed body and the long arms made Scarne aware that the other man watched him, too, with a slight, crooked grin. Scarne pushed against the back of the seat, glowering, the fight gone out of him.

Silence settled on the coach. The girl gave Blaise a swift smile in silent thanks. Then she turned to the window again.

Now Blaise noticed her. She would be tall, slender. She had smoky-blue eyes, and the hair beneath the pert hat and veil was a dull, coppery color. The planes of her face were strong and yet the structure seemed delicately molded. She wore a striped, tailored coat, a small gold watch pinned to one shoulder. A heavy brooch relieved the severe white of her waist and lace collar. As little as Blaise knew about such things, he saw that her clothing was expensive. He sensed wealth and assurance.

But she held his attention only for the moment. Looking out the window again, he saw landmark after landmark pass. Places and things that had played a part in an old life, but were now almost as strange as this world he had entered after long years of exile.

His thoughts moved ahead, ranged back into time and his dark eyes grew more somber. Immersed in a world of his own, he was no longer conscious of the coach, the passengers, the dust. The girl coughed.

He looked around. Scarne had lit a cigar and the strong blue smoke whipped past the girl and out the window. Scarne's full lips worked at the cigar and the smoke grew thicker. The girl coughed again.

Hal leaned forward and took the cigar from Scarne's fingers. The man stared at him in amazement as Hal studied the smoking weed and then flipped it out the window. He waited, balancing easily against the constant jolting of the stage.

"Mister, you learn hard," he said. Scarne's lips opened to protest but he caught Blaise's steady gaze. He subsided, muttering under his breath. The girl held a handkerchief to her lips, but her shoulders shook and her eyes danced.

The road turned sharply to the north, heading directly for the mountains. It began to climb and the low hills closed around them. The slopes grew steeper and now the coach almost crawled. At the top of the grade the driver reined in the horses, set the brakes. Blaise opened the door and stepped out, stretching, looking around at the close-pressing hills. The road lifted just ahead to another ridge, and then it would enter Cahuenga Pass before dropping into the great valley beyond.

Hal King joined Blaise. He was perhaps half a head shorter, a solid, stocky man with a violently freckled face and blue eyes that at the moment looked guileless. He shifted his gun and holster to a more comfortable position and then stared around at the hills.

"Greasewood and sagebrush, wild oats," he said in a lazy drawl. "They don't look like much."

"You'll see, Hal. In twenty more miles we'll be there."

Hal lifted his hat and wiped the sweat from his forehead, then ran his fingers through his red hair. "None too soon, Blaise. It's been a long, mean trip." He looked back at the stage and the men on the high seat. The guard sat at ease, smoking a cigarette, but the twin muzzles of the shotgun across his knees conveniently pointed toward the two men who stretched their legs.

"We're carrying something this load," Hal said. "That guard ain't taking no chances."

6

"Interested?" Blaise asked softly.

"Hell, no!" Hal exploded. "I've had more'n a crawful of that." Then he grinned. "You're hoorawin' me."

"Sure," Blaise said and turned back to the coach when the driver lifted the reins.

The girl had taken Blaise's seat and she looked up at him, her glance a hopeful question. His wide lips relaxed slightly, hardly a smile, and he sat down beside the salesman. The driver yelled stridently, the whip cracked and the stage lurched forward.

The big horses stretched themselves now and the coach swayed as it picked up speed. The hills pressed in and the passengers could see only the ragged, dark green carpet of the sage, the more waxy tone of the sumac.

Blaise's thoughts raced ahead, down the miles of dusty road to journey's end. There'd be a girl who had waited for him. He tried to shape her picture in his mind and it came so clear that he knew it could not be wholly right. Ten years had passed and she'd be . . . let's see now . . . close to twenty-eight. She'd have eyes like lupin, soft as its dainty petals, golden hair that caught a man's eyes and held them, that invited the caressing touch of his fingers.

He moved restlessly at the vivid picture. Blue and gold and fair white skin. The girl opposite him was dark, lovely in her way . . . but not like Melanie.

The road lifted again as the hills pressed closer. There was a last steep grade and then the driver halted the horse for a blow. Blaise half opened the door and leaned out, some of the somber look gone.

7

"The Valley," he said to Hal. "It's good to see it."

The girl looked up, alert. "Do you live in the Valley?"

He hesitated. "Intend to, I reckon."

"Where?"

Blaise made a slight, vague gesture with his hand. "Somewhere. Don't rightly know yet."

He closed the door and settled back, looking out the window again and effectively blocking any further conversation. Her lips half parted in anger.

The road dropped steadily to the floor of a wide valley. The mountains dropped away to the left and then paralleled the road. Far across the Valley floor another range of low mountains lifted. Between the ranges spread rich grassland, a bright green now so soon after the rains. Far to the north, a larger range shoved sawtooth peaks to the sky where even yet the sun flashed on distant snow.

Blaise watched, impassive face hiding the excitement that stirred within. His eyes drank in the scene as though he had thirsted for it all these weary years. The San Fernando . . . his valley, his home. Then doubt muddied the thought and the excitement died as uncertainty swept over him. At one time, he had striven mightily to sink his roots here. But now? . . .

The road reached the level of the Valley floor and the sweeping panorama of the moment before was gone. But still the eye followed the long waves of grass on and on, to the northern range. Now and then ancient oaks broke the wide sweep, old and twisted trees that had seen the first explorers, perhaps Portola, and the mission fathers. Twisted and old, they gave Blaise a subtle sense of patience and peace. He had always liked the oaks.

Hal King watched the Valley in honest curiosity. He studied the grass, the slight lift of the land, noted the brush that marked what might be watercourses.

The stage slowed as the driver applied the brake. The coach swung off the highway to a stage station. He dropped from the high seat, announcing there'd be a stop for dinner.

Blaise climbed out and stretched, his big hands in the small of his back. Across the road was a sheep pen and Blaise turned swiftly, looking to the south, recognizing this as a corner of the old Encino ranch.

The station itself was a low, squat frame building with a sagging roof. Just before it stood a hitchrack along which stood eight saddled horses, heads dropping in the warm sun. The other passengers had left the stage and walked to the building. Hal came up and stood beside Blaise, looking around.

"I think I'm glad I come along. It's rich country." Then he frowned, turning his head in a long circling look. "But I ain't seen much beef for all this grass."

Blaise shrugged. "It does look empty. But that's a lot of valley for cows to roam in, and the hills can graze a lot, too. There's beef, Hal. The Spanish run 'em by the thousands and the mission had near as many."

Hal dismissed the thought and squinted up against the sun at the shotgun guard. "Don't you ever eat, mister?"

The guard gave him a wary, searching glance and smiled reservedly. "In time, friend, in time."

Hal grinned and followed Blaise to the building. They stepped inside. The place was large. A zinc bar stood to one side, a few tables, a long plank one for eating and, beyond them, a few for poker games, empty now.

The bar was lined with men, riders with the dust of a long trail on them. Blaise glanced toward the tables, rejected the thought of food, and turned to the bar, Hal following him. They took their places, two of the riders giving them surly looks as they made room.

Blaise realized then that some of the men were Mexican, all of them wore gun belts. He ordered drinks from a bartender who moved as though pins pricked him at every step. Blaise nursed his drink, became more aware of the men around him. They looked hard, something reckless in each tanned, dark face. Hal leaned closer.

"You have salty riders in these parts," he said in a low voice.

Blaise looked carefully down the bar. After all these years, Leonis must still have his gunhawks and border breeds. The bartender jumped when one of them banged his whisky glass on the counter. Blaise watched, eyes narrowing. The man had something worrisome on his mind. Blaise turned slowly and leaned back against the bar. The passengers sat at the table, served by the proprietor and a shapeless woman who hurried from kitchen to table. Blaise noticed that they threw quick, apprehensive glances toward the bar.

One of the riders stood out from the rest, a tall, slender man with an air of command about him. His eyes were large and dark, full and mobile lips beneath a thin mustache. His face was gaunt and bony, and black curly hair escaped from under a low-crowned dusty hat. He wore levis, scarred boots and a soiled shirt, the color faded to a faint suggestion . . . typically American and yet, somehow, Mexican, too. He wore a heavy gun belt around his thin waist. There was something tense about him, an ill-concealed wildness that showed in the quick, erratic smile, the way his eyes moved about the room.

He saw the girl from the stagecoach and his smile flashed wider. Her chin lifted slightly in the gesture Blaise had come to know.

The driver finished eating and came to the bar for a drink. Blaise caught the quick signal that passed from man to man. The riders hastily downed their drinks and walked outside, swaggering a little. Blaise straightened, sensing something wrong. One of the riders moved from the bar to the door and leaned negligently against the frame. Blaise nudged Hal, who looked around the almost empty room.

The proprietor had stopped midway from the kitchen to table, his face frozen, eyes stricken. Blaise and Hal turned together and instantly the man at the door drew his gun in a swift, smooth motion. The girl gasped and Blaise froze as the black gun muzzle swung toward him.

"You will be very still, *señors* . . . and *señorita*. There will be no harm, I think."

A gun blasted outside and instantly the shotgun roared a deep, throaty cough that slapped against the walls. More gunshots came in quick succession. Hal's eyes widened.

"Be damned! A holdup!"

His hand rested close to a whisky bottle. He grabbed it, and hurled it at the man at the door in a single, flowing motion. At the same time, he threw himself away from the bar. The guard half turned, saw the bottle hurtling toward him and ducked. His gun hand twisted and the Colt thundered in the room, the bullet digging splinters from the wall beyond the bar.

Blaise slipped to a half crouch and his hand dropped to his Colt. The weapon snapped up, fell back in his palm and bucked as he pulled the trigger. The slug cut a long splinter from the doorframe and made the bandit jerk away.

Hal threw himself in a flying tackle, coming in low and fast. His shoulder struck the man in the stomach as his arms wrapped around him. They hit the wall with a shaking thud and the bandit's gun flew from his hand.

Blaise stepped in, waited a second until the bandit's head was exposed. He brought the gun barrel down in a single, chopping blow and the fight was over.

He turned to the door. Hal stepped clear and jumped to the nearest window. He broke out a pane with the gun barrel as Blaise jerked open the door.

He saw the guard sprawled in the dirt beside the coach. Two of the bandits held the horses, and two more lifted a heavy box from the boot. The handsome fellow had sat his horse near the hitchrack, and he had twisted about to face the building. Hal's bullet lifted his hat from his head.

Blaise fired, dropping one of the men with the strongbox. His next shot spun the second man half around. Hal's gun roared from the window and another bandit dropped from his horse.

Bullets smashed into the building and Blaise ducked to cover. Hal fired twice more and then dropped below the window as lead smashed the glass in a shower of crystals. Bottles broke behind the bar.

Blaise caught a man racing from the coach to the hitchrack. His gun jumped and the man's legs went rubbery as he plowed face forward into the hard ground.

"*Vamose! Vamose!*" The harsh voice lifted in a strident order. Blaise stepped into the door again. Riders milled around the rack. A bullet clipped close to Blaise. He crouched and his shot toppled another man.

The bandits suddenly broke from the rack, racing away around the corner of the building and out of sight. The sound of hoofs thundered loud and then faded away toward the mountains to the south.

Hal slowly straightened. He swung out the barrel and ejected bright shells to the floor, grinning at Blaise.

"A sudden country," he drawled. "You didn't tell me that."

"Hadn't thought about it," Blaise answered. He stepped out into the yard, Hal following him. The driver pulled himself from behind the overturned table and ran cursing after them.

Two men were dead, another sat with a smashed shoulder, moaning softly. The driver hurried to the guard and turned him over. He blinked and shook his head, looking around and up at Blaise.

"Three bullets," he said in quiet anger. "Any one would've killed him. Bob never had a chance."

Blaise nodded, face set. "They paid for it and you've got two left alive to hang."

"By God, they will!" The driver stood up. "I'll see Bill's taken care of, and lock them two up for the sheriff. But I ain't got a guard."

"Go without one," Hal suggested. The driver turned, angry.

"Mister, it can't be done. That strongbox carries money from a Los Angeles bank to one in Buenaventura. We got to —" He stopped, eyeing Blaise.

"You'll do, friend, the way you handle a Colt." He added swiftly, "It'll only be to the relay station in Conejo Valley. The Company'll see you won't lose."

"No," Blaise shook his head. "You don't want me. Get one of the other passengers."

"Hell, man! Did any of them stick his nose out the door? You're it, mister, and I wouldn't want better."

Blaise's lips flattened and a bleak look came in his eyes. He shook his head. "There's two things against it, *amigo*. First, I'm only going to Calabasas —"

"Ten miles further, maybe," the driver cut in. "We'd loan you a horse —"

Blaise's lifted hand stopped him. "Second, *amigo*, would you trust your strongbox with a San Quentin jailbird?"

The driver blinked. "You?"

14

Blaise nodded and turned away. The driver caught his sleeve.

"You're still guard for my money. Someone made a mistake, I reckon. Never saw men could handle guns as fast as you and your partner. Here, mister. You got a job . . . and a reward as soon as I can tell the Company what happened."

He pushed the heavy shotgun into Blaise's hands and turned back to the station, calling for help to patch up the wounded and clean up the yard. Blaise weighed the shotgun, looking as though he had never seen one before.

"Looks like you're elected," Hal said.

Blaise grunted and shook his head. He laughed, the sound deep at first and then fading away. He glanced at Hal, his lips in a crooked grin.

"A funny world, Hal, when a murderer and a robber guard a strongbox. But who ever made much sense of it, anyway?"

CHAPTER
TWO

The stage left the station an hour late. As the driver settled himself in the high seat and picked up the reins, Blaise tapped him on the arm.

"You're sure you want me? My kind ain't hired for responsible jobs."

The driver spat over the side of the coach. "I've noticed that sometimes thieves ain't penned up and a good man gets jailed. Ain't asking no questions and don't have to. You handle a gun to my taste and you look right to my eyes."

His whip snapped and the horses settled to the pull. Blaise shrugged and placed the shotgun across his knees, reaching in his shirt pocket for his tobacco sack.

They wheeled out to the main road and started westward. Blaise started his smoke, pulled his hat brim lower against the brilliant sun. His eyes swept southward where the Valley floor sloped to the first low ridges lifting to the area of jumbled peaks and crooked canyons that formed the mountains.

The bandits would have no trouble at all in that country, he thought. He followed the line of the ridges westward where the mountains closed in, choking off the Valley. The driver broke in on his thoughts.

"That must've been Vasquez," he said. "And it's the first time he couldn't pull off a job."

"New to the Valley?" Blaise asked.

"Brand new. He come from up north a year ago, but he's been operating south of the mountains."

Blaise watched the Valley. He had been afraid that it might have changed, but it hadn't. Far across to the north he could see the peculiar rock formations of the Santa Suzannas, tawny in the sun. The sky was blue and clear, blending magically with the deep, dusty green of the sagebrush hills that subtly changed to rusty purple. The wild oats stood tall and green now. Later they would wither and the dust would film over everything so that a man might believe this a stricken land. But the rains would come, the heavy, steady downpours, and the snow would gleam on the distant mountains, and the whole miracle of vibrant life springing from death would be repeated again.

It was good to be back, good to see that nothing had changed. It was still serene . . . except for that little pocket to the west where Calabasas lay. But man had changed that . . . man, and greed and a lust for power. Blaise's lips slowly pressed and the soft light faded from his eyes. Perhaps that would be unchanged, too.

"You live in these parts?" the driver asked.

"Used to, years ago."

He was not gruff, but his brevity discouraged conversation. The driver watched the road for a long while before he tried again.

"Thought you might live somewheres close. Maybe I could get you a job riding shotgun guard for the line. It pays good."

"I couldn't get the job if I wanted it," Blaise said. "Forget it, friend."

"Hell's bells, you'd at least take a reward, wouldn't you!"

Blaise grinned. "Might."

"Then where'll they find you?"

"Right now, I'd say Calabasas. But it might be a thousand miles away . . . or boothill. *Quien sabe?*"

"You go right well with the sunshine and the flowers," the driver grunted.

As they approached Calabasas, climbing over the Chalk Hills, Blaise straightened, showing more interest. He watched the mountains to the south now, eyes darting to a ridge, resting a moment, picking out a peak further on, then another.

"Good country," he said half aloud. "Good cattle country."

The driver turned, giving him a long, surprised look. "Since when, mister?"

"Always was."

"Have you seen a cow since we dropped into the Valley? There ain't been cattle to speak of for I don't know how long . . . more'n the five years I've been on the run."

"Gone? . . . five years!" Blaise's jaw dropped. "Why?"

"A drought that killed cattle off like flies." He slapped the reins. "Only Scorpion runs cattle and

18

damn' few head at that. It just ain't good business no more."

Blaise stared ahead, eyes narrowed. "Scorpion! Leonis still run it?"

"Hercule Leonis, that's right. A big man in these parts, but a bad'n to cross. Maybe you knew him?"

"Maybe," Blaise said.

"Never saw the man myself. But I heard . . ." He noticed the fierce turmoil in Blaise's eyes, the way a muscle jumped in the lean cheek. The driver studied him closely and felt a slight shiver that was akin to fear. "Almost to Calabasas now. Sure I can't talk you into riding on . . . or taking the job regular?"

Blaise shook his head and then looked up, smiling. "Not for a while. I might go into the cattle business."

The driver blinked. "But —"

"It's no good," Blaise finished for him. "I know, but neither am I."

He squared around in the seat. The driver gave full attention to the road and the stage rolled steadily on, both men wrapped in silence.

They approached the far end of the Valley. Blaise saw a glitter ahead, the reflection of sun on glass, and then he had his first glimpse of the town. His fingers tightened on the shotgun and then relaxed. There lay journey's end, and the beginning of a new life. The buildings grew larger — the old store, unchanged, to the left of the road and, beyond it, a huge oak tree. The blacksmith shop, the hotel to the right with the wide, shady veranda apparently had not changed, nor the few houses scattered along the first gentle slopes that lifted

19

to the hills. Beyond and above the town stood the low ridge over which the road climbed to the Conejo Valley.

It was as if his memories had suddenly come alive. They reached the first scattered houses and a dog came racing out to bark excitedly at the coach. The driver pulled back on the lines, kicking on the brake. He turned off the road and they came to a dust-rolling halt before the store. He leaned down and shouted in the window below.

"Calabasas. You got time to stretch before we roll on."

He climbed down, then called up to Blaise. "Give me that new carpetbag right behind you under the tarp, will you?"

Blaise found it and pitched it to the driver. The girl had descended and stood beside the driver, looking up at Blaise. She was beautiful . . . it struck Blaise forcefully. For the first time, he saw her as a person worthy of attention.

She smiled up at him. Blaise took off his hat. "I must thank you," she said, "for all of us. You were very brave."

"Oh, now —"

"But you were." Her eyes danced. "And my personal thanks for protecting me all the way from Los Angeles."

Blaise chuckled. "It was a pleasure . . . and easy. If Mr. Scarne played poker, he'd've known a bluff when he seen one."

"I wonder." She became serious. "If you're staying in Calabasas, I hope to see you."

"It will be a pleasure, ma'am, though I don't really know how long I'll be around."

She smiled again and turned away, picking up her carpetbag. Blaise jumped from the seat to help her. Hal chuckled and Blaise swung around, his face growing red. Hal leaned against the coach, rolling a cigarette. He licked the tube of paper and indicated the girl.

"Pretty as they come, though I ain't exactly a judge of women. And money, too, from the looks of it. That team of blacks ain't to be bought out of a puncher's wages."

Blaise turned. A tall man, dressed in checked shirt and levis had come up to her, respectfully touching his hat. He took the bag and placed it behind the seat of a shining black surrey. The team that drew the buggy had not been bought in this part of the country. They were coal black with the lines of Arabian and Morgan in them. As Hal had said, no ordinary puncher and very few ranchers could have afforded such a matched team.

The man helped the girl into the surrey, climbed in the seat and lifted the reins. The buggy rolled away in a cloud of dust, heading southward toward the mountains. Blaise stared after it, then shook his head.

"Now there was a rich girl for you, Hal. Your troubles would've been over."

"She wouldn't see no one but you," Hal said.

"You could've told her I got me a girl waiting," Blaise grinned. "You ain't quick to turn things your way."

Hal looked beyond Blaise. He remained leaning against the coach and his voice didn't lift.

"How quick are you, Blaise?" Blaise caught the slight, urgent tone in his voice.

He turned. Six men walked steadily toward him. They had apparently waited for the coach at the blacksmith shop. Five of them Blaise didn't know, five hard-eyed men who walked with their hands swinging free near holstered Colts, five who watched him warily as they approached. They came in a half circle that converged on him.

The sixth Blaise knew, and felt again the terrific impact of the sheer size of the man, a feeling he had not known for a decade. Leonis still towered head and shoulders above the ordinary man. Blaise was tall, but he still had to lift his eyes to meet Leonis'. And he was wide with his height, wide and solid, like a mountain that could move.

Hercule Leonis, owner of Scorpion, had once claimed mastership of the whole Valley that stretched twenty miles eastward and ten to the north. And he had controlled it with violence, with guns, with fire, with arrests and jail, with bought judges and juries. Now Blaise faced him once more and his hand instinctively lifted to his gun.

Instantly the five dropped into a crouch, hands held slightly outward, fingers clawed above smooth walnut handles, eyes narrowed and lips flattened against their teeth. Leonis stopped, huge, square face impassive, heavy lips slightly pursed. His voice rumbled deep in his chest.

"You have come back, Randell."

Blaise nodded. "I'm back." Suddenly anger swept him. "Pardoned, Hercule. You couldn't buy a governor, could you?"

"You speak foolish . . . now, like you did then." He glanced at Hal, who had straightened and had edged toward Blaise to back him against the five. The big man's lips curled.

"You have returned to Calabasas. You will leave again. The stage will take you."

Blaise shook his head. "Guess again, Hercule. You railroaded me out once."

"I do not guess. Return to the stage. It will take you away, safe and alive. If you do not, then we shall see what is to happen."

"He ain't fooling," Hal said in a low voice. "Give me the two to the left and the one in the middle."

Blaise motioned him to silence. The giant waited patiently. Blaise sensed the loafers who stood beyond the line of fire on the far side of the store. It had always been that way. When Leonis walked the town, the rest stepped aside, giving him the street.

"There is no place for you here." Leonis said abruptly. "There has been peace since you left, but you will bring us trouble . . . like the old days."

"You've had peace and I bring trouble!" Blaise exclaimed, his voice mocking. He balanced on the balls of his feet, his attention centered solely on the giant. His voice tightened. "You had it because you drove every decent homesteader and rancher out of the Valley one way or the other. You pinned a murder charge on me. I paid ten long, killing years for something I didn't do. I swore I'd come back and find the straight of that killing, Hercule. Here I am. I'm coming back to people I know, to land I own. Can you stop me?"

Leonis shrugged. "There are no people you know here any longer. They have gone across the mountains to the Conejo or the Simi Valley."

"All gone?" Blaise demanded.

"All," Leonis nodded. "None of them are left. You did not see a place as you came along the road, eh? Nothing between the road and the hills above the pass at Chatsworth? They once tried to build the homes, eh? Where are they now?"

Blaise waited. He sensed Hal beside him. The five gunhawks stood frozen, also waiting. Only Leonis moved, swinging one giant arm in a half circle toward the hills.

"The Valley is empty. Calabasas is quiet now, and that is good. I think that maybe five men are not enough that maybe you go. So there are others hidden so . . . and so."

The stage driver lifted his voice from the canopied porch of the store. "Hey, you can't chase that man out! He broke up a robbery at the Sheep Pen station."

Leonis shook his head. "That I am glad to hear. But still he goes. Perhaps there is no law in Calabasas, as they say, but the town will not have the murderer return. He leaves."

Leonis turned but the five men hardly batted an eye, still as coiled snakes. Blaise suddenly laughed, a mirthless sound that brought Leonis to a full turn. For

24

the first time he showed signs of anger, his chin jutting his eyes flashing.

"It is funny, eh?"

Blaise nodded. "It is, in a way, this welcome-home party. You'll always have your gun hands, Hercule, you'll always depend on force . . . Nothing else."

Leonis' face cleared and he gave a shrug that was pure Gallic. "It has always worked. It always will. I learn that when I was a boy herding sheep in the Pyrenees. I learn it when I come to America and then to California. You see how it is now. There is you, there is me . . . but you are alone. I have men. Who will live the longest, eh?"

Blaise considered it. "A point," he conceded. Leonis made an impatient gesture and turned to the driver.

"You are late. They will expect you at the next station." He threw his ultimatum over his shoulder to Blaise as he walked away. "You will leave Calabasas, Randell, by this stage. My men either see you leave or drop you in the dust."

He strode on, unhurried, a huge and majestic man. Ruthless, Blaise thought as he watched him, a man always sure of himself. Blaise turned to the five men. They still waited. He heard Hal stir behind him.

"How you calling it?" Hal asked.

Blaise thought of hurling a challenge after Leonis. But it would mean nothing. The big man would not even look back. Blaise's lips tightened and instantly five men grew tense.

"We'll look over Conejo," Blaise said softly, then lifted his voice. "But I'll be back."

"We'll be waiting," one of the five said.

Blaise climbed up in the high seat. The driver scurried to the coach. The five gunmen still waited. The driver picked up the reins, lifted the whip from the socket and it cracked like a pistol shot. The stage rolled out into the street.

They passed Leonis. Blaise stared straight ahead, though the big man turned, looked up. Hal leaned out the window and his shout carried above the noise of the rattling stage.

"We'll be back, friend. We'll be back."

Leonis replied but Blaise could not hear him. The stage rolled along the street through the town and started climbing to the low pass ahead.

Blaise realized his hand was clenched so tightly that the knuckles showed white, and his breath was deep, angry, gusty. He threw a quick sidelong glance at the driver, who spat elaborately over the side.

"I like a man that uses his head though he's plain fighting mad. You'll get another chance at that big jasper. Don't know but what I'd like to be around, too. Giddap, Silk! You, Mose! Git along."

CHAPTER
THREE

Blaise scowled ahead at the saddle of the pass, thinking bitterly that his return to the San Fernando had been brief and to no purpose. The top of the grade was close now. Blaise looked over the top of the stage back along the road. Three men followed just beyond Colt range. Blaise knew them to be Leonis' men. He had an impulse to jump down and challenge them. Being forced to leave the town was bad enough, but to be escorted from the Valley was worse.

Blaise fought down his anger. The long years in San Quentin had taught him nothing if not patience. He eased back in the seat, staring moodily ahead.

The coach reached the top of the pass and rolled along the winding downgrade. Just as they rounded the first curve, Blaise looked back again. The three riders stood lined against the sky. One lifted his arm in a mocking salute, wheeled his horse and turned back to Calabasas. The other two turned more slowly as the stage rounded the shoulder of the hill.

Blaise straightened again, fighting down a new surge of anger, his fingers clenching the iron seat brace. The road curved again, still dropping, then leveled across a small meadow before it snaked around another moundlike hill. The horses were running easily now, the stage rolling smoothly. The driver cuffed his hat back and spat again.

"You've got one man that hates you complete and thorough, friend."

Blaise said nothing and the driver shook his head. "And he throws a wide loop in this part of California. I'd worry some if a man like that was after my hide."

Blaise snapped, "You let me worry . . . if I want to."

"And welcome!" the driver exclaimed, "though I've heard tell he's had trouble lately."

"Trouble?" Blaise lifted his head.

"What I heard. Nothing you could put your finger on, except whispers and guesses. He ain't fighting and grabbing like he used to, I hear."

Blaise slightly lifted one eyebrow. "When Leonis stops grabbing, the North Pole will get warm."

"Maybe, maybe . . . like I said, it's just what I hear. Most likely there's nothing to it."

It seemed to Blaise that the run to the next station would last forever. He still smarted under the affront at Calabasas and now he wanted to be off the stage, to find Melanie and his friends, to feel that at last in some small measure he had placed the grim years at San Quentin farther behind him.

He could see and feel the hard walls again, the narrow cell. The long, gray and aimless days passed again, the sense of futility and numb revolt like a lead weight on his mind, the dismal dungeons. He remembered the long first nights when over and over he had tried to understand why he had been adjudged guilty and sentenced on such flimsy evidence.

A man had been killed in Chatsworth, a man with whom Blaise had admittedly quarreled. But Blaise had been riding the Santa Monica canyons when it had happened, riding alone. On his return to Calabasas he had been seized by Leonis' gunhawks, thrown into a barn for safekeeping overnight, and then driven to Los Angeles for formal arrest.

Blaise had written to Melanie and her father, Paul Case. They had appeared, along with some of the others who had been fighting off Leonis' attacks on their Valley homesteads. But they could only testify to Blaise's character. The prosecutor proved that none of them had known Blaise's whereabouts at the time of the killing. It had been very easy then to show motive and even opportunity on the strength of his absence. Leonis had been behind it . . . Blaise knew that. The man had power, he boasted of owning judges and juries.

Blaise served ten years before a new governor had miraculously pardoned him. Long before his release, Blaise had sworn that he would find who had actually done the murder and that he would break Leonis. He didn't know how, he just knew that he would.

He grunted angrily as he twisted in the seat. On his first meeting with the big Frenchman, he had been bested, ordered out of town and an escort sent along to see that he left. Blaise's face grew warm and he writhed inwardly.

They approached a village and the stage station was just ahead. The driver wheeled the horses off the road and stopped the coach exactly before the entrance. Men came out to unhitch the horses and lead them to the big stables. Fresh teams were brought up.

The station itself was a combination hotel, café and bar, a long two-storyed building, white and clean in the shade of the big oaks. Blaise climbed down from the seat, following the driver.

"I rode further than I intended," he said shortly. "How much do I owe?"

"Owe! Hell, man, nothing! We owe you!"

"Forget it."

Hal stepped out of the coach. Blaise saw his slightly raised brow, but he only shrugged and turned to the station. Hal fell in step beside him. He spoke in a low voice.

"Blaise, when did San Quentin turn a man loose with a pocketful of money? Or maybe I didn't get my share."

"Why take a reward?" Blaise looked squarely at his friend. "I didn't see you waiting to find out what your pay would be."

"Impulsive . . . you'll see that more'n more."

"You'll fit in this country," Blaise said dryly. Hal chuckled.

"I think you're right." They entered the building and saw the dining room to the right. They found a table and gave their order to a harassed waitress. Hal leaned his elbows on the table.

"Speaking of impulses, I figured you'd jump those five back in Calabasas. I was thinking what I'd say to St. Peter in about a minute."

Blaise grinned. "Think he'd listen — or you'd even get there?" He sobered and looked darkly across the room. "But someday I might even the tally when I know more of what's happened."

He studied his fingers, his forehead deeply creased.

"Something's changed, Hal. I can see it and feel it. Leonis is still a powerful man and he won't stop at anything. He was always that way but . . . why hasn't he grabbed up all that Valley land? Why didn't we see a single head of beef from Cahuenga to Calabasas?"

Hal shrugged. "Summer pasture up in the hills?" he suggested. Blaise shook his head.

"No. This ain't like northern Arizona or Montana, or even like Sierra country. There's nothing gained by moving herds."

The waitress brought their food and Hal pulled closer to the table. Both men ate swiftly, with a strange intensity. They had just finished when the driver came up to the table, another man with him.

"This is the gent," the driver said. "That changed Vasquez's mind."

The man instantly shoved out his hand. "I'm Kennedy, division manager for the stage line. You saved us a lot of money, Randell. We appreciate it. I'm suggesting the Company give you a reward. Leave your address and I'll see you get it when it comes through."

Blaise stood up. He grinned, his eyes mocking. "Address? *Quien sabe?* It might be this town, or

Calabasas . . . or hell. You can look for me any of those places. But my thanks, anyhow."

He signaled to Hal. A moment later, they stood outside watching a new driver climb up into the high seat of the coach, pick up the reins, and the coach rolled down the highway toward distant Buenaventura. Hal looked across the road at the single general store, the saloon and the livery stable. The dark, rolling hills lifted beyond.

"Now what?" he asked.

Blaise sighed. "Blamed if I know. Maybe we can figure some way —"

He stared across the road toward the store. The door had opened and a woman stepped out, carrying a bundle toward a buggy hitched close by. Blaise's eyes widened, lightened, and suddenly he raced across the road. Hal turned, surprised.

Blaise circled the buggy, halted a few feet from the girl. His eyes drank her in, the sky-blue eyes that had opened wide at the sight of him, the corn-gold hair that escaped from below the little hat with the single flower, the long, narrow face with the high cheek bones, the skin as fair as the sunlight.

"Melanie!"

The bundle slipped, she caught it. Her lips moved soundlessly for a second.

"Blaise!"

She said it in whispered wonder. Her eyes skittered beyond him, across the road, to the store, back to him. "You — you can't be here. You . . . did you escape?"

"Escape!" Blaise laughed. "Didn't you get my letter? I've been pardoned. I'm free as the air, Mel! Lord, I've dreamed of seeing you just like this.

He took the bundle from her slack hands and then kissed her full on the mouth. He dropped the bundle and pulled her close in a long and hungry kiss. The girl placed her hands against his chest, slowly pushed him away. She couldn't quite look directly at him. It took her some time to get her voice.

"I — Oh, Blaise, I —" She laughed. "You took me so by surprise. What will people think?"

"People?" Blaise asked. He chuckled. "I'd forgotten about that. Mel, you're more beautiful than ever. I thought you were still in Calabasas."

"No . . . we left there . . . years ago, just after you were . . . went away." She looked beyond Blaise's shoulder, startled. Blaise turned. Hal stood at the end of the buggy, rolling a cigarette, watching them.

"Hal, meet Melanie. Remember, I told you about her?"

Hal smiled and took off his hat, his hair gleaming coppery in the sun. "I thought this was her, Blaise. She's just like you said."

"Hal King, Mel. He came down with me. I told him we could work the ranch together, get it started and going again."

She opened her lips, closed them, then turned to the buggy. "You'll find things changed, Blaise . . . terribly changed. Get in. We'll go home. Dad and . . . Walt will be glad to see you."

"Walt, that little shaver! How is he?"

"Fine. But he's eighteen now and almost as tall as you."

Blaise felt the jolt of it, the realization that the years had passed him by. People had gone on living, growing, changing, dying, while stone walls had enclosed him in a gray limbo.

"I'd forgotten," he said quietly and helped Melanie into the buggy. Blaise climbed in, took the reins, pressed close to her so that Hal could find a seat. "Which way?"

"Turn north at the next road. We're five miles out."

Blaise slapped the reins and the team stepped out. He turned right at Melanie's signal and soon the town was behind them. The dirt road led almost straight to the first low mounds, then described a wide loop around them. This valley was smaller than the San Fernando and more broken by a series of low, rolling ridges, a beautiful, and peaceful land. Even Blaise felt a sense of security.

Hal watched the countryside, seeing it with a cowman's eyes, prejudiced at the sight of furrowed fields, regretting that the rich loam showed where good grass should stand knee high. But he was more interested in the girl, more than he cared to admit.

He watched her from the corner of his eyes. He felt that the girl hardly knew what to do, that Blaise's sudden appearance had presented an urgent and hard problem to her. Hal was puzzled, knowing Blaise had always dreamed of marrying her. Hal wished he could be as lucky someday.

"You really wrote?" Melanie asked.

34

"Sent it to Calabasas," Blaise nodded. He took her hand. She started to withdraw it, then let it lay passive under his own. He was puzzled and he looked questioningly at her.

"Glad to see me?"

"Very glad. It's been such a long, long time."

There was no real enthusiasm in her voice. Blaise considered that she might still be surprised at the sudden sight of him, and he turned the conversation.

"So you left the San Fernando. You never mentioned it when you were writing regular."

She caught the implication and gently withdrew her hand. She spoke as though she talked of someone else.

"It was Leonis. About three months after you . . . left, he made open war. We were burned, shot at from ambush and finally his hoodlums raided us. We could never prove it was him, of course."

"Who ever could?" Blaise grunted.

She sighed. "It finished us, though we drove the raiders off. We knew there'd be more raids, more burnings. Leonis would never let us stay on land we had filed on by law. The whole Valley was his —"

"I know," Blaise cut in gently. "I was in that trouble, too."

"I forgot. Who should know better? Anyhow, Mark . . . you remember Mark Davis? . . . Mark and some of the others thought it best if we let Leonis have the whole Valley if he wanted it. Even Dad thought it would be wise." She made an all-inclusive gesture. "So we came over here. We've been left alone and most of us have proved up on our homesteads. The land is ours."

Blaise's eyes darkened again. He could see the sudden attacks, a barn flaming high in the dark night, and hear the crack of a rifle from some rock outcropping. He had known the same thing himself before Leonis had shipped him safely off to jail.

"It's more than time," he said tightly, "that Leonis is called to taws."

"It can't be done, Blaise," Melanie shook her head. "He was a big man when you left. He's even more powerful now. He's the king of Calabasas."

"We had a sample," Hal said dryly. Blaise explained. Melanie listened, not at all surprised.

"He *is* too big," she said. "You can see that."

"Maybe," Blaise answered stubbornly. "Say, how about that ranch of mine up in the hills?"

"The buildings still stand, but they say Leonis uses them as a work camp and they're all run down."

"We'll change that," Blaise said, "Hal and me." He looked across Melanie, grinning at the red head. "I guess we're still in the cattle business."

Melanie shook her head. "Your beef's all gone, Blaise. Leonis kept us busy taking care of ourselves. I guess they strayed or were run in with other herds."

"More can be had," Blaise said cheerfully. He looked around at the fields, the plowing contoured to the hills. "Must be plenty of farmers in this part of the valley. Where does your range begin?"

Melanie hesitated. "We're farmers, Blaise."

He blinked, turned, eyes aghast. "You're — what!"

"Farmers. Dad, Mark, all the old bunch you knew. There was a drought eight years ago. It lasted two years

36

and wiped almost everybody out. The old ranchos went under and the little cattlemen never had a chance. Cattle died of starvation. There was nothing left of the business."

"That's hard to take, Mel."

"One ranch up beyond the Mission had five thousand head left standing out of two hundred thousand," Melanie said. "It hit Leonis hard, nearly wiped him out. That's why he's left us alone, I guess."

"They didn't tell me in prison," Blaise said. "Maybe the newcomers thought I knew. So it hit Leonis?"

"Hard," Melanie nodded. "But he's making a comeback, now that the market's opened and new people are coming into Los Angeles. He'll be one of just a few to run beef. Cattle on a big scale in this part of the country is done."

They had come to a series of low hills and threaded the gentle pass between them. Now the hills fell back and ahead lay a valley that was narrow and crooked. Here was the heart of the region. Plowed fields lay dark and neatly fenced under the clear blue sky. Blaise saw scattered buildings, each group marking a farm. It was lovely, pastoral, but not at all to a cowman's taste.

Melanie pointed to a house not far distant, a white one with a red roof, shaded by huge trees. Barn and neat buildings clustered about it.

"We live there."

"A new home," Blaise said. Melanie laughed.

"Hardly that any more."

"I keep forgetting," Blaise said quietly. He added. "I wonder what happened to my Valley homestead."

Hal looked surprised. "A ranch . . . and a homestead?"

"I filed on Valley land adjoining the ranch. That's when Leonis figured I'd stepped on his toes. I never had a chance to prove it up. It's gone now."

"We abandoned, too, Blaise," Melanie said. "Mark proved it was the wise thing to do."

"Mark — Mark Davis," Blaise said, remembering. "I'd almost forgotten him. We were always on opposite sides of the fence. He never wanted to fight from the beginning."

"He was right, Blaise," Melanie said in a strange voice. "Everything worked out just as he said it would."

Blaise distastefully moved his lips. "Sure, but I was never one to let another man drive me. Mark never gave a hang for principles — it was always results with him." Blaise grimaced. "Maybe he was right after all. I went to jail and he moved over here. He's set up good, I reckon, the best land of all?"

"I . . . yes, it is the best," Melanie replied slowly. They were much closer to her house now. The paint was new and gleaming, the fences in good repair. Blaise glimpsed a stout corral where a couple of saddle horses and several, powerful work horses stood. Melanie broke in on his thoughts.

"Blaise, I . . . the first years after you left were hard and terrible." He looked around but she stared straight ahead, talking a little faster. "We did what we could in the other valley, but Leonis was too much. We moved, and we had all the hard work of building and starting new over here."

"You've done a good job," Blaise said.

"No one thought you'd ever come back. We knew what Leonis could do and . . . some even thought maybe you *had* killed Chavez. You'd had trouble with him before."

"I never liked the man — a thief, a liar, and crooked as they come. But I never killed him. I intend to find out who did."

"After all these years?" she asked.

"What else is there to do?"

"Nothing, I guess," she said. After a short pause and a swift, almost frightened glance toward her home, she continued. "There was only trouble for us and we thought you'd never come back. People do unexpected things sometimes, Blaise, at a time like that."

"Like following Mark over here," Blaise said. He turned the buggy into the farmyard and looked around in grudging admiration. "You've prospered."

He turned the buggy about in the yard and reined the horses in beside a stone walk that lead through a little gate to the smooth green yard around the house.

"Where's Paul?"

"Dad . . . lives up the road."

He looked surprised. "Up the road! But you don't run this place alone!"

A man came out of the house. He paused on the step, looking at the buggy and then he came slowly to the gate.

Blaise recognized Mark Davis. The years had been kind to him. Only faint shadows of lines from high-bridged nose to full mouth marked increased age.

He was still handsome, a tall and heavily built man. He wore levis, a checked shirt, but there was hardly any mark of the farmer about him. After his first, startled glance at Blaise, his dark eyes slid away as they used to do.

"He's back, Mark," Melanie said in a strained voice. "He got off the stage as I was in town. You remember Blaise?"

"I remember him," Mark said evenly. He watched Melanie.

Here was another change whose proportions Blaise did not know. It was a threat; he could sense it in Melanie's strained voice, in the ill-concealed antagonism of Mark Davis. Blaise mentally braced himself. For a long, long moment no one moved. Blaise, Hal and Melanie sat stiff and quiet in the buggy, Mark stood at the gate, his hand tight around the top bar, face set and hard.

Melanie stirred and forced a laugh. "Well, we can't sit here all day. Mark, aren't you going to invite our friends in the house."

Blaise grew tight with a cold, numb feeling of disaster. Melanie stirred and Hal abruptly jumped out of the buggy and helped her to the ground. She still smiled, but her eyes were frightened as she looked at Blaise.

"Light down! Welcome to our home."

"Our?" Blaise asked with difficulty.

"Of course! Mark and I are old married people now." She turned to her husband. "Mark, aren't you glad to see Blaise after all these years?"

CHAPTER
FOUR

Blaise remained still, his eyes shadowed and a mist filmed them. Melanie swallowed a hard constriction of the throat and he read something unspoken and appealing in her eyes. He looked at Hal and to Mark.

The man still stood at the gate, watchful. He smiled as he read Blaise's face and strode through the gate placing his arm around Melanie's shoulder, pulling her close. His voice lifted, almost boomed.

"Why, of course I'm glad to see him, honey. Light down, Blaise. Is this your friend?"

"Hal King," Blaise said automatically. "Maybe we'd better get on. I didn't know . . . that is, I ain't sure —"

"Nonsense! You can spend the afternoon, anyhow. Light down. I'll unhitch. Honey, you take 'em into the house."

He patted her shoulder and hugged her close again. Blaise reluctantly wrapped the reins around the whip socket. Hal lifted the grocery sacks from the back and handed one to Blaise. It gave Blaise something tangible to hold onto. They followed the girl into the big and airy kitchen.

Once inside, the girl turned swiftly. Blaise somberly shook his head.

"Mel, you should've told me."

"But — but, I . . . couldn't. I tried to stop writing but your letters came and I —" she lifted her hand and let it drop, "I had to write anyhow."

"But this?" he demanded harshly. She turned away and stood by the table.

"I tried, Blaise. I started a dozen times and tore up the letters. It was too — cruel."

"Cruel?" he asked dully. She whipped around.

"Blaise, can't you understand! You were gone, for good — like as if you were buried and you'd never come back. Everyone told me that — everyone . . . Dad, Mark, all of them. I —" She looked toward the window and her voice dropped. "Here comes Mark. I'll — explain later. Please, Blaise."

He turned to a big dark cabinet in the corner and methodically lifted the packages and cans from the sack. Mark entered in a rush, pulled up short when he saw Blaise at the cabinet, Melanie at the wood range across the room, Hal lounging easily by the table.

He pulled out a chair, whirled it around and sat down, arms over the high back. Blaise carefully placed the groceries on the cabinet, sensing Mark's searching stare.

"You look about the same, Blaise. Little gaunter, maybe a little thinner in the face." Mark tipped his head slightly. "You don't have that old hellion spirit. Maybe they took it out of you."

"Mark!" Melanie turned, shocked. He threw a glance over his shoulder.

42

"What's wrong? It's true, ain't it? Look at him yourself."

"It's true," Blaise said heavily. He looked about the room as though it had suddenly become another cell.

"Sure, Blaise, anyone can see it. Surprised about me and Mel?"

"Yes."

"She should've told you." Mark fished a tobacco sack from his pocket. "I always had my eye on her, Blaise, but you had the inside track in the old days. You don't blame me?"

"No," Blaise looked at Melanie, a long glance that swept from the crown of her head to her toes. He passed his hand wearily across his face. "Where does Paul live?"

"Down the road — the next farm. Why?" Davis asked.

"Maybe Hal and me had better get on down there."

"Hell, you'll stay here!" Davis stood up. "At least until supper time. Honey, cook a supper that'll show Blaise what he missed. Come on, gents. This way."

He would not listen to their protests and finally Blaise followed him. The bedroom was high-ceilinged and spare, looking out toward the road. Mark left them there and Blaise strode swiftly to one of the tall, narrow windows.

He looked out toward the hills, across the plowed fields. His hand gripped the casing. Behind him bed springs squeaked slightly and Hal spoke in a low voice.

"Changes . . . always changes."

Blaise could feel the dampness in his eyes and he had to swallow. "Why did she do it?" he asked. "For ten years she was all that kept me going up there. Just two things I wanted to do . . . get out of jail and come back to her. I'd swear if anyone in the whole damned world would've stayed beside me, she would."

Hal asked, "Did you tie her down before you left?"

Blaise shook his head. "No . . . I said nothing."

He shoved his thumbs into his gun belt and his eyes moved along the rhythmic swell and dip of the hills. Now he saw it as Melanie must have, and he realized how unfair he had been. They had only hesitantly spoken of marriage to one another, but not to anyone else. Both of them had been so caught up in the turmoil of the trial that neither of them had thought of anything else. Blaise had not seen Melanie after he had been taken from the courtroom. Leonis had seen to that.

Blaise sighed and much of the turmoil left him. "You're right, Hal. She had a right to look for someone else."

"Life imprisonment," Hal arose from the bed. "Like she said, what's the difference between that and being dead?"

He came up beside Blaise, who rolled a smoke and inhaled deeply, looking out the window again, this time seeing the gold and red sunset on the rim of the hills.

"I feel lost, Hal. Nothing's like it ought to be — nothing."

"Give it time to straighten around, *amigo*. You'll see where you stand." Hal turned to face the room. "The

44

bed looks soft and maybe we oughta get some rest at that."

It was sensible. Blaise stretched out on the bed, with his hands beneath his head, staring up at the ceiling. Fatigue flooded his body, but he couldn't sleep. He was too aware that he rested in Melanie's home. A couple of times he felt the flood tide of loss sweep over him, but he beat it back. Hal had been right. He could rightfully expect nothing. She had done what she had to for good and sufficient reasons, even to choosing Mark Davis. This house, the farm, everything pointed to his ability to get along in the world.

Blaise was glad when Mark knocked on the door and called that supper was ready. They ate by lamplight in the big kitchen. Melanie had dressed for the occasion and Blaise felt a deep pang every time he glanced across the table at her. Hal frankly watched her.

"We'll ride down to Paul's after supper," Mark said. "You'll be a surprise, Blaise."

"It'll be good to see him."

Mark ate awhile and then leaned back in his chair. "Things have changed, Blaise. They finally followed my advice and moved over here into Conejo. We've prospered, all of us that dug in and worked. It was a wise move."

"Was it?" Blaise asked. Mark laughed.

"We're in peace. We're prosperous. We're left alone. More'n you could say of San Fernando in the old days."

"You're left alone because Leonis wants to leave you alone," Blaise answered slowly. "If he decided to take over Conejo, would you give up again and move out?"

"Now that's a damn' fool question!" Mark exploded.

"We'd better hurry to Dad's," Melanie said hastily.

Melanie and Mark rode in the front seat of the buggy, Mark's back stiff and straight. Hal and Blaise rode in the back, Blaise trying to watch the night rather than Melanie's slender shoulders.

A dog barked as Mark wheeled the buggy into the Case yard and a man came to the door, holding a lamp high above his head. Melanie called.

"It's me, Walt. Tell Dad and Mom we've got a big surprise."

The four of them walked to the porch. The man with the lamp held the door open. He was about eighteen, man-sized, except for a face that would fill out in time, and long awkward arms. He had Melanie's blue eyes and corn-silk hair, a golden fuzz on his cheeks.

A woman exclaimed, "Land sakes! It's Blaise Randell! Oh, son, you're good for these old eyes!"

She held him close, kissed him, then held him at arms length, fondly looking him over. Mrs. Case had gray hair now but her plump face seemed just as smooth as ever. Paul Case took Blaise's hand in a strong, friendly grip.

"I'm glad to see you, boy. We never expected to . . . this *is* a surprise. When did you come?"

There was excited babble and Blaise felt the warmth of old friends who had never changed. They asked a hundred questions. Blaise introduced Hal as his partner in starting the old ranch again. A silence fell.

"You'd be a fool, Blaise," Mark snapped. "I could find some good rich land this side of the mountains. You could do as well as the rest of us."

Blaise shook his head, his lips pressing together. "I had a ranch when I left. If Leonis grabbed it, then I'll get it back." He laughed to break the tension and turned to the boy who stood against the far wall.

"This is Walt?" he asked of Melanie. "You'd never believe he was a towhead squirt in bare feet when I last saw him. It's good to see you grown, Walt."

He held out his hand. Walt flushed fiery red, grinned and awkwardly accepted. He met Blaise's look squarely and studied the man before him.

"I remember. You ain't changed none, sir." Blaise thanked him with an extra pressure of his fingers.

They finally settled down, catching up on past history, mentioning names that Blaise had almost forgotten. They were careful not to ask Blaise about his prison life. He put them at ease by frankly speaking of it. Several times Blaise caught Melanie's long regard and the sense of loss cracked through the impersonal wall he tried to build so rapidly between them. Young Walt listened with his eyes gleaming as the talk turned to the old days when Blaise and the others had fought Leonis. Paul Case leaned back on the horsehair divan and sighed.

"But now what will you do, Blaise?"

"It could depend on you."

"Here we are," Paul said.

"Farmers?" Blaise asked and saw the old man flush. "Cattle and open range are too much in your blood, Paul. I never thought you'd stop fighting Leonis."

Mark Davis made an impatient sound and Maw Case looked frightened. Mark struck a match along his levis, lit his cigarette and looked angrily at Blaise.

"You paid for fighting him. We saw what happened to a man who didn't have sense enough to quit." Melanie's eyes widened and she looked hastily at Blaise, then down at her hands. Mark exhaled noisily.

"We leave Leonis alone. He leaves us alone. We're getting ahead. What's the use of you coming in and stirring up trouble?"

Blaise looked from Mark's angry face to Paul. The old man rubbed his jaw, slowly, his forehead creased, and the lamplight accented the trace of the years. Walt sat on the floor by the wall, hands around his knees, face alight, his eyes jumping from one to the other. Blaise spoke evenly.

"Maybe time has made a difference with you. But I've had a million hours to think of Leonis and what he did. He drove all of you out. I can understand that maybe you'd pull away for a time until you figured you could go back and call him."

"Foolish! Crazy!" Mark muttered. Blaise swung around to face him directly.

"Is it? You were whipped clean out of the Valley. You were driven off land that belonged to you by every right . . . You think that's forgotten? Do you think Leonis would wait a second if he decided to take over this land? A man has to stand up for his own

48

rights. Once he runs, he'll run a second time . . . and again . . . and a third time. It works that way."

"He's right!" Walt exclaimed. All of them turned to look at him. He blushed, wriggled uncomfortably and managed an apologetic grin. Mark looked sidelong at Blaise.

"It's good talk for young'ns, Blaise. It's hot-head talk, it's mad talk because you've had nothing to do but hate Leonis all these years. But we've been busy. We've built over again. We got something. You want to tear it down. It'll only get you behind bars again."

"Now, Mark —" Maw Case objected. Blaise smiled at her.

"Maybe he's right, Maw. He was never one to fight when it'd be easier to pull out and get ahead." Blaise shook his head as Mark made an angry gesture. "Who knows which of us is right, Mark? You see it one way, me another. But I won't let Leonis brand me a killer. I've got to clean that up."

"But — it's so long ago!" Melanie protested.

"I still carry the brand. Sure, the governor decided the evidence was thin, too thin to hold me for life. He pardoned me."

"What more do you want?" Mark demanded. Blaise's brow lifted.

"The easy way again, Mark? I was pardoned . . . get it? — forgiven for a killing I didn't do."

"So you're pardoned," Mark sniffed.

"But I ain't cleared," Blaise snapped. "I intend to find out who killed Chavez. I aim to haul him in and make Leonis admit he railroaded me. I can't let a murder stain follow me all the rest of my life. Freedom ain't worth it."

They were all silent. Hal took elaborate care in rolling a cigarette, secretly watching the rest of them; Maw's look of understanding pity, Melanie torn between the man she married and the man she should have, Walt's eager response to the adventures and excitement he sensed not far off, Paul's slow, troubled thoughts.

"But I'm going to need help," Blaise said at last. "I've come to folks I figured could give it. How about it, Paul?"

Case jumped, startled. He glanced at Maw, saw Mark's set chin. All of them waited as he weighed one factor against another.

"Blaise, we know you didn't kill Chavez. We're satisfied, like all your old friends will be."

"It's not enough, Paul."

"I know," Paul admitted and added reluctantly, "but I'm along in years now. Mel's married, Walt's coming on. We've put all we've got in this place and — old people get tired, Blaise. All that fighting is years back."

"You won't help?" Blaise asked in surprise.

"*I* will!" Walt exclaimed, and he came to his feet. He disregarded his father's startled look and Mark's swift anger.

"I'll do all I can, Blaise."

"Sit down, Walt," his father said quietly. The boy deflated, aware of his bony wrists and awkward legs. He sat down again. Paul looked straight at Blaise.

50

"I'll help, Blaise. You know that. But I won't start no range war again. I won't risk having Scorpion riders killing and scorching here like they did in San Fernando. Up to that point, you can call on me for anything. What do you need?"

Blaise recognized determination and immediately accepted the limited offer. "That'll do, Paul, for now. Where is the old bunch?"

"Most of them are up toward Simi — Joe Malin's here in Conejo, but Joe's half blind now. The Freyn brothers left the country."

"How would they feel toward Leonis?"

Paul hesitated, but Mark cut in. "They want to leave him alone — like the rest of us."

Paul shrugged. "I guess Mark's right, though I don't rightly know."

"I'll talk to 'em," Blaise decided. "I'll see what they know, how they feel. There must be some who'd like to even the score with Leonis."

Mark slapped his hands on his knees and arose. He looked down at his wife. "We'll be getting home. It's late."

Blaise glanced, startled, at the clock on the far wall and arose himself. Mark faced him coldly.

"Blaise, I don't want you at our house. You're too dangerous . . . to me, to Paul or any other man that wants to live peaceful. Ride somewhere else . . . far away. Leave me and mine alone, leave all of us out of your plans."

Blaise paled and Hal hastily edged out of his chair, standing balanced on the balls of his feet. But Blaise spoke quietly at last.

"It's how you say, Mark."

Mark nodded shortly and his jaw thrust forward. "While we're naming spades, Blaise, I'll call another one. Don't try to stir up trouble in Conejo. I'll fight you every way I can, and no holds barred. Good night and — I hope — good-bye."

Blaise looked at Melanie. She stood, the fabric of a handkerchief taut between her fingers. She looked utterly miserable. Blaise read the turmoil and pleading in her eyes. Mark turned toward her. She flushed, started to protest but instead dropped her head and walked toward the darkened bedroom to get her bonnet.

"Blaise," Paul said hastily, "stay with us. There's plenty of room and you're welcome."

"Land sakes, yes!" Maw Case surged up from her chair.

Blaise and Hal remained while Paul and his wife went outside with the others. Blaise traced the faded rug pattern with his boot toe. Hal watched, sighed deeply.

"You know where you stand."

"I always knew, with Mark," Blaise answered. "It's nothing new."

"The others?" Hal asked dryly.

"I don't know. They'll follow Mark, I reckon. I've got a one man war, looks like."

Paul and Walt came in, and Blaise heard the buggy rattle away down the road. Paul made talk while Maw prepared the guest room. At last she came to the door and said it was ready. Her eyes softened when she looked at Blaise.

"Pay no 'tention to Mark. Sakes alive, he's just plain stubborn mad." Her voice softened when Blaise looked up with a twisted smile. "You didn't know about him and Melanie? . . . I told her to write you time and again, but she wouldn't. Said it would do you no good. I — I wish —"

"Maw," Paul said quietly. Her eyes misted. She turned and hastily left the room, leaving the men in an embarrassed silence. Blaise tugged at his ear lobe, broke the strain.

"I'll take some air before bed."

"Right off the kitchen to the right," Paul said, hesitated and then added flatly, "Good night."

Blaise walked out into the yard. The stars blazed down and the hills were only dark, silent shadows. He lit a cigarette and walked to the far end of the yard, leaned on the fence overlooking the road. A pinpoint of light came on far away in the night and Blaise watched it, dragging deeply on his cigarette. Melanie and Mark . . . Melanie. Someone moved behind him and Blaise turned to find Hal standing a foot or so away.

"You," Blaise said and looked again at the distant light. He spoke quietly. "Things happen . . . Everything changes."

"Sure, it's always that way," Hal answered. "A man's a fool if he expects the world to stay as it is."

"Only Leonis," Blaise said. "He's the same . . . yet." There was a long silence between them. Hal leaned on the fence. Just then the distant light winked out. A mockingbird sang dreamily from somewhere behind the barn and a vagrant wind stirred lightly and was gone.

"You're still going after him?" Hal asked.

Blaise turned impatiently. "What would you do?"

The silence grew long between them before Hal sighed. "Make someone pay for ten years stolen right out of my life." He straightened. "But don't rush it, Blaise. If I was Leonis, I'd be waiting for you to make one wrong move. You'd go right back to San Quentin."

Blaise flipped his cigarette over the fence. It showered sparks and snuffed out.

"Not this time. Not twice. I'll be dead first."

CHAPTER
FIVE

The next morning Blaise and Hal both awakened at the first sound of stirring in the house. It was still dark but there was a feeling of dawn not far off. Blaise sat up, startled. He heard Hal stir and chuckle.

"Jail habits, Blaise. When'll we wear 'em out?"

Blaise sighed, scratched his head, then yawned widely. He swung his feet to the cold floor and started dressing.

When they entered the kitchen, Maw Case worked at the stove, alone in the big room, cheery with lamplight. She looked surprised.

"Land sakes, whyn't you sleep! No need for you to get up. Paw and Walt can take care of the chores."

"Habit, Maw," Blaise explained.

"Well, a good one," Maw said, breaking eggs in the skillet. "Washstand's outside just beside the door."

The air was chill, typical of the California nights, and the water cold enough that it drove the last shreds of sleep away. The stars blinked brightly in the sky but to the east there was a faint hint of gray. A lantern bobbed from the barn as Paul and his son came to the house.

They went inside and sat down to the table, loaded now with eggs, bacon, biscuits and coffee. They ate silently. Paul finished first, crossed his knife and fork on the plate and leaned back in his chair.

"Ain't changed your mind, Blaise?" he asked.

"No. How about you?"

"No use, Blaise, even if I did. We're well out of the old trouble."

Maw Case left the kitchen as Blaise rolled a cigarette. He spoke with elaborate casualness. "How come Melanie and Mark got married?"

"You should know, Blaise. A girl can't wait for a man that's as good as dead. You had a life sentence."

"I can understand," Blaise nodded. "But Mark? I don't savvy that."

Paul shrugged. "Mark has his faults, but he's as smart a trader as I've seen in my time, and he's a careful, saving man."

"He always was . . . careful," Blaise said dryly. Paul said nothing. Blaise toyed with the coffee mug. Paul seemed to feel that something more need be said.

"They've been married a little over two years now . . . happy enough."

"I dunno," Walt cut in. "Sometimes I think Sis ain't —"

"Walt, I'll do the talking," Paul snapped. The boy subsided, glowering at his plate. "Maybe there has been a little trouble now and then, but married folks always have it. I — I think I know how you feel, Blaise."

"Do you?" Blaise asked with sudden fierceness and then subsided with a twisted grin. "Maybe you do at that, Paul."

56

"I once hoped you and her would be married," Paul continued. "I thought of you like a — a second son. But I was one that urged her to marry Mark. Maybe I done wrong, but it was best as I saw it at the time."

Blaise pushed away from the table and arose. "It's still best, Paul. Mark's got a heap to offer. I'll get used to it in time. I — I hope she's always happy, Paul."

"She will be."

After breakfast, Blaise and Hal helped with the work around the barnyard. Walt stayed close to Blaise, shadowing the older man, eager to explain about the most insignificant thing. But Blaise drew the line at ploughing.

"It's like tearing up good grass for nothing."

"Things have to grow so people can eat," Paul suggested, "and ranching's dead in this part of the country."

"Sure, but I got too much cattle in my mind and blood."

Paul started off to the fields, Walt reluctantly following him. Blaise and Hal returned to the house. Maw Case kept them busy for another hour, catching Blaise up on ten years of news.

At last Blaise escaped to the bedroom. Hal came in soon after. Both men stretched out on the bed. Blaise listened to the muted sounds from the kitchen, a bird singing just outside the window. Hal sighed.

"I like this country. It's a place for a man to live."

He stared dreamily out the window, the light accenting the strong line of the chin and the bony irregularities of the freckled face.

"Now I see it's no place for a puncher," Blaise said abruptly. "It'd be better in Arizona."

Hal shook his head. "People back there'll never forget I run with a wild bunch and landed in a California jail. No, this is best."

"There's no ranching," Blaise warned.

"Not enough to keep a bunch of big spreads going like used to be here," Hal said thoughtfully. "But with all the folks in Los Angeles and more coming, I figure you and me could make a go of it. Leonis is. Why can't we?"

"I see it that way. But we can't depend on anyone but ourselves. That'll make it tougher. Maybe you won't like those odds."

"If you'd come back alone," Hal asked, "would you have given up by now?"

Blaise considered the question only a moment. "No."

"Well, two men were always better'n one," Hal said. "You've still got a partner."

Right after the noon meal, Blaise busied himself in the barn, working over a harness. Hal had saddled a horse and had ridden northward up the Valley road on a leisurely exploring trip. Blaise worked slowly, checking the leather, mending and oiling. His thoughts mulled over the factors that had changed and reshaped his plans.

He couldn't be too sure of anything, except that he'd leave the Conejo in the morning. He wanted to get away. He now thought of the ridges and mountains above the San Fernando almost as a place of refuge. He could rebuild in those hills, make the past dim, perhaps reorientate his life.

He heard a buggy come into the yard and he stood up to look out the dusty window of the harness room. Melanie climbed out of the buggy and Blaise stood transfixed. He could look at her without encountering her strange, apologetic glance, the troubled shadows that came to her eyes.

She stood for a moment by the buggy, a tall and lovely woman, her beauty a torture. He felt that he looked at two girls; the Melanie who stood by the buggy looking toward the barn, and the Melanie who had been in his thoughts for so many long years, a beautiful and tormenting vision during the long and lonely hours. The two were strangely blended and yet separate.

Melanie turned to the house. Blaise sat down again. He didn't want to see her, so he concentrated on the leather.

He looked up. She stood in the doorway, watching him. There was something soft and appealing in her uncertain smile.

"You keep yourself busy," she said. Blaise stood up. She stepped into the room and sat down on a three-legged stool. Blaise rubbed his palms along his trousers.

"Where's Mark?" he asked.

"In the fields."

"Why did you come here?" Blaise demanded harshly.

Anger flared in her voice. "This is my father's house."

"Does Mark know you've come?"

Her eyes dropped and she looked toward the window. Finally she answered in a faint voice. "No. He . . . doesn't want me to see you again."

Blaise could see the curve of her cheek, the shapely neck, the rise and fall of her full breasts beneath the calico dress. He moved back to the door, leaned against the frame.

"Then why did you come?"

It took her a long moment to answer. "To see you . . . to explain about Mark and me."

"You married him," Blaise said carefully. "I've heard all the reasons and thought up more for myself. It's been sudden for me, but all the same, I hope you and Mark are happy."

She turned, quickly, and then caught herself. He had an impulse to walk across the room and take her in his arms, to hold and kiss her. Something of his turmoil must have showed in his face for she looked hastily away.

"There was something else," she said. "I'm afraid for you."

"For me?"

"You're going to fight Leonis again." She made a swift gesture as his face fell. "It's dangerous, Blaise. It was bad enough when all of us were together. But you'll be alone now."

Blaise crossed to the window, making a slight circuit around her. His fingers beat an impatient tattoo on the ledge.

"What would you want me to do, Mel?"

"You could forget the past, Blaise. You could start all over again — something new. There's land to be had here or up in the Simi. It'd be better than going back to the San Fernando Valley."

"You'd want me here — in this valley?"

Red touched her throat and cheeks and then faded again. "I would rather see you here than in jail again, or dead. Oh, Blaise, I can see how you feel toward him — all of us do, Dad, Mother, Mark, all the rest. But that's past and done. Leave Leonis alone now, and he'll leave you alone. He has all he wants."

"All he wants," Blaise repeated. "But how am I branded? Murderer!"

"We've had peace," she said and stood up, taking a step toward him. "Now you'll bring trouble to us again. It'll start out just your fight, but you'll pull us into it. We've gone through one range war, Blaise. It's horrible. We can't go through another."

Her hand touched his arm. She was close and Blaise looked down into her eyes. They stood transfixed, and her lips grew soft, slowly parted. Blaise lowered his head and his hands reached for her.

Abruptly he dropped them and his head jerked up. He strode across the room to the door, turned to face her.

"I'm leaving in the morning. I'll see how things are." He paused and his fist clenched, but his voice lowered. "I won't be seeing you again, Mel."

"Blaise!"

He hurried out of the barn, and walked to the corral, hooked his elbows over the top rail and stood there, eyes closed.

He wanted to go back; every nerve called for her.

But he held himself tight to the rough, wooden rail. He could go back — he knew it. But where would it lead? He heard the rattle of the buggy as it turned in the yard and drove off. The sound faded away and there was only the faint sigh of the wind.

He remained where he was, staring blindly at the ridges that barred off the San Fernando. She was gone . . . back to Mark . . . for good. It was best.

He cursed, deep and strong.

CHAPTER
SIX

It was still dark. Blaise tightened the cinch of the saddle. Lamplight lengthened Hal's legs and put Paul's sober face in a weird half light, deepening the eye sockets and making a hawk's beak of his nose. Walt moved swiftly, placing a saddle on his own horse.

Paul looked up toward the eastern sky. "Dawn before long, and a clear day. Walt'll take you to Simi and bring the horses back."

"Let me ride on with 'em, Dad," Walt asked. Blaise cut in before Paul could reply.

"Not this trip, son. Later, when there's more important work to do, we'll call for you."

Paul looked thankfully at Blaise. "Only chance of trouble is beyond the pass," he said, "between there and your ranch."

Blaise made an impatient sound. "I'm against this. It's like running from Leonis."

"This ain't running." Paul shook his head. "No use riding direct through Calabasas when you know Leonis will have his boys looking for you. This way, you'll be on your own land before Leonis can do anything about it."

"He's right, Blaise," Hal said. Blaise turned to the horse and gathered the reins.

"All right. Let's ride." He swung up into the saddle and then leaned down, holding out his hand. "Thanks to you, Paul, for putting us up."

"No bother at all. Glad to have you. Come around when you can."

"Not for a while."

Paul looked steadily up at him. "Melanie. You'll get over it."

Blaise straightened. He nodded to Paul and touched his heels to the horse. The three men rode out of the yard, hardly more than looming shadows against the dark sky.

They threaded a series of low hills as the sky lightened, became gray and then erupted with the whole glowing spectrum of sunrise. It bathed them in a rose and golden glory that gradually changed to full yellow glare.

The three worked through the hills and came into the Simi, another long and narrow inland valley bounded by the hills and mountains. Their way joined the main east-west road at a small village that was no more than a store, a livery stable and a scattering of houses.

Blaise made inquiries and the three rode half a mile to the north. Blaise and Hal spent the next hour dickering for two saddle horses, plain saddles and bridles.

Walt watched glumly as Blaise adjusted blanket and saddle on his new bay gelding. The animal was powerful and would absorb a great deal of work. Hal's was a gray, almost the size of Blaise's.

"I feel like I amount to something," Blaise said with a grin. "A man's lost without a horse."

"They're good mounts," Walt said grudgingly. Blaise turned to face the boy.

"The trail forks here, Walt. We sure thank you for coming with us. Tell your dad we thank him, too."

"Sure you don't need a hand?" Walt asked and his face dropped when Blaise shook his head. He sighed and spoke impulsively. "I'd sure be proud to work for you, Blaise, from what Dad used to tell about the old days."

"Paul always liked tall yarns," Blaise grinned, came over to the boy and put his hand on his knee. "But I'd be proud to have you with me. I'll let you know as soon as I can."

Walt lifted the reins and slowly turned his horse. He rode away, leading the two extra mounts. He twisted around in the saddle, lifted his hand and then turned into the road that led back to the Conejo.

"He'll make a man," Hal said quietly. Blaise nodded.

"If there'd been more like him ten years back, things might've been different."

Hal spoke softly. "I have an idea there was. But somebody changed 'em."

Blaise looked at him. "When did you learn to read my mind?"

"From picking over my own," Hal laughed grimly, "when there was nothing else to do but look at stone walls. Let's head for your ranch."

They mounted and rode eastward down the Valley. It was pleasantly warm. The hills wore a new emerald green and gradually Blaise's spirits rose in response to the sparkle in the air, the joyous color of the hills, the fleecy clouds floating high above. Hal whistled under his breath and Blaise hummed a snatch of the song with him.

"Good to be living again," Hal said.

"I'd almost forgotten how it was," Blaise answered.

In a little over an hour they came to another crossroads village. Ahead of them, pushing a huge rock barrier across the Valley, stretched a chain of yellow-rock mountains, bold and forbidding. A huge freight wagon stood before the store, the six horses lazily switching flies. They glanced at the store as they started to ride by, saw no one around the door or the huge wagon. Blaise looked toward the mountains trying to recall the last time he had ridden this way. Suddenly the store door slammed like a pistol shot.

"Blaise!" a roaring bull voice called. "Blaise Randell!"

Blaise twisted around, his hand dropping to his holster. A man had jumped off the store platform and came running to them. Blaise's face lighted.

"Slim Starling!"

He vaulted from the saddle as Starling came up. Big, sinewy hands grasped Blaise's shoulders and shook him. Slim stood a good two inches over six foot, a handsome bear of a man with black, unruly hair and a flaunting hawk nose in a swarthy face. He nearly lifted Blaise from his feet.

"You old horse! I knew they couldn't put you away for good! Hey! We got to have a drink for this one!"

Blaise managed to introduce Hal, who winced when the big man shook hands. Slim made a wide gesture.

"This calls for plenty of powwow, Blaise. Where were you heading?"

"The old ranch."

"You'll run smack into Leonis and he'll try to trim you to size again. Leave him alone, Blaise."

"I've already run into him." Blaise told of the meeting in Calabasas. Slim shook his head and led the way inside the store.

There was a clear space in the back, room enough for a small table. Slim sat down on a box and told Blaise and Hal to drag up seats. He bought a bottle from the proprietor, opened it and poured into tin cups.

"To the old days — when there was guts in this part of the country! And damnation to Leonis!"

Blaise lifted his cup and took a short swallow. Slim drained his, banged the cup on the table and wiped his lips with the back of his hand.

"So you come back. I thought they had you put away for good."

"Pardon," Blaise said shortly. "After I could get the governor to look at the evidence."

"Now what?" Slim asked. Blaise shrugged.

"Back home again." He added after a pause. "I've been in the Conejo."

"The old bunch," Slim's lips curled. "I don't think there's much of a man among 'em."

"Paul Case is getting old, the rest have scattered."

"Sure — but what about the others? Hell, I was as hard hit as any but I'd've stayed right on fighting Leonis if the rest would've stuck. We was raided a couple of times, but Leonis was finding it too damn' costly to keep it up."

"Was he?"

"Some of his boys was left both times and more carried bullet holes back with 'em." Slim speared a thick finger at Blaise. "That was land open for filing, wasn't it?"

"Yes."

"And all of us filed legal, didn't we?"

"So far as I know."

"Then how in the name of roaring hell could Leonis get away with what he did? I told Paul Case and Mark Davis to take our troubles to the U.S. Marshal, and damn the crooked judges in Los Angeles. They wouldn't . . . leastways Mark said it was no use and the rest didn't argue with him."

"That might have worked," Blaise nodded.

"Leonis gave you a legal bushwhack," Slim continued. "Then I said that we could move into that high Box Canyon among the rocks of the Santa Susannas. You could hold off an army there, and we'd see that none of Leonis's men or cattle roved the Valley range. Mark said that was crazy, and the rest fell in with him. Anyhow, they all moved out. I couldn't fight Leonis alone, so I went along with 'em."

"To Conejo?"

"Me farm! Slim Starling push a plow!" He grinned. "The drought came not long after and nobody run cows any more. Even then I be damned if I'd watch the hind end of a horse across a field. I took to freighting. Been doing it ever since, between Gomez Station, Los Angeles, Fillmore and Buenaventura."

"Mark Davis swings a wide loop," Hal said quietly. "Why?"

Slim scratched his chin. "I don't know — never did know. He could talk a badger out of his hole. He was right, he knew it, he told you, and you was a damned fool otherwise. It'd always make my hackles raise, but I never did nothing about it."

"You left land belonging to you," Hal insisted.

"Sure, but what good was it? How could we get anywhere when half the time we was fighting night riders and the other half we was watching for 'em? That's what Mark said — and he was right. We could get further by just letting Leonis have it. He was right again, for the folks in Conejo have done real well. But I still wanted to stick on."

"That's the way I felt," Blaise said soberly. "And now I want to go back."

Slim twisted around and squinted out the door. He scratched his head and ran his knuckles along his jaw, at last slapping the table with his palm.

"Be damned if I don't help you! I'm sort of wasting away in peace and quiet these days."

"But your job —" Blaise started and Slim's roaring laugh checked him.

"When was I ever tied to any job, Blaise? I've got a load for Gomez Station and a return haul to Fillmore. When I finish, I'll saddle a horse and ride over to see

69

how you're coming along. If you need me, I'll stick around. If you don't, I'll ride back to Fillmore and freight again."

"You're asking for trouble," Blaise warned. Slim dismissed it with a wave of his hand.

"No more'n you, ranching right next to a man that hates your innards. I heard a rich jasper from the East has bought up a heap of that mountain land. He don't like neighbors close. You could lock horns with him."

"Who is he? Where's his spread?"

"Up in the hills somewhere close to your old place. I heard his name's Thatcher, but that's all I know."

"We'd better get along," Blaise said as Slim poured another drink around. He finished it, arose and dropped his hand on the big man's shoulder. "You'll be welcome, Slim. It'll be like old times."

"You be careful," Slim warned, "until I get there. We'll give Leonis something to really worry about."

He walked outside with them and moved up close to Blaise when he mounted. "Did any of the Conejo folks talk about Chavez?"

"No," Blaise shook his head. Slim made an impatient gesture with his hand.

"That gent deserved killing, but I never figured you done it. It wasn't like you to sneak up on a man, Blaise."

"I intend to find out who did it."

"It's a cold trail," Slim shook his head. "I wouldn't bet a bent peso on your chances."

"I can try." Blaise straightened and Slim stepped back.

"I'll help you when I finish this haul. Take care of yourself until then."

Blaise touched spurs and Hal rode thoughtfully beside him, studying the high rock escarpment. The valley pinched in and the road turned to find way between two low mounds, precursors of the broken country ahead. Hal turned, resting a hand on the horse's rump as he looked back toward the distant store and the wagon. He straightened, glanced at Blaise.

"That jasper had a point," he said abruptly. "People can forget a lot in ten years."

Blaise's jaw tightened. "I'll find out."

"Leonis?"

"— or one of his men," Blaise added. "It comes to the same thing."

Hal shook his head, pursing his lips. "Maybe . . . maybe."

They climbed up into the mountains, the road narrowing to follow the canyons. At times it was little more than a wide ledge high along canyon walls, again it would emerge into brief flats surrounded by tier on tier of yellow rocks, wind and weather eroded into a myriad fantastic shapes, clinging miraculously to the vertical slopes. Except for rocks and sagebrush, the mountains were barren. The rocks trapped the heat of the sun so that it concentrated balefully on horses and riders.

Now and then, they had brief sight of the great sweep of the Simi Valley behind them, but soon that disappeared as the mountains pressed in. Hal lifted his hat and wiped his sleeve across his forehead.

"Useless country," he decided aloud. "Wouldn't feed nothing but snakes, and damned few of them, I bet."

Blaise laughed. "You might be driven up here if things get too hot for us in the Valley. You could hole up forever if you wanted to."

"Had to," Hal corrected. "I can't figure anyone wanting to come up here."

They reached the high point of the road and it began to drop in long, curving loops down along the mountain sides. Now they had glimpses of the San Fernando, in huge vistas that took the eye the whole length of the Valley, to the far distant Verdugo Hills and the tremendous San Gabriel peaks behind them. But always the rocks closed in, shutting them off from the wider world, trapping them in a blaze of sun and yellow rock.

They finally broke through the mountains and drew rein atop the last ridge. The road followed the crest for a short distance and then looped downward to the Valley floor. Not far away in a pocket formed by the mountain range stood a cluster of houses.

"Chatsworth," Blaise pointed to the village. "We'll have to trade here for supplies if Leonis keeps us out of Calabasas."

"Where's your ranch?"

Blaise pointed southward to the distant line of mountains across the sky.

"Over there."

"More mountains," Hal said dryly.

"Not like these. You'll see."

They rode across the Valley, alert and ready for trouble. Now they invaded land originally claimed by Leonis, but they met no riders. They crossed the main stage road and headed directly for the mountains just ahead. In a short time they were hidden from the Valley by the sheltering ridges.

These Santa Monicas were quite different from the chain to the north. Hal saw it instantly. There was still sagebrush, still a jumbled, tip-tilted land. But there were fewer rocks and more meadows between the peaks, horse-belly deep in grass. This was truly cattle country, though broken.

Blaise led the way without hesitation, cutting along the ridges toward the west and south. They came on a narrow trail, half overgrown. Blaise drew rein, looking around slowly. Every ridge and slope was familiar after all these years. The trail lifted to a notch betwen two peaks. Just beyond, he knew, it would widen into a pleasant canyon and the house would be on the slope just to the left. Hal watched Blaise, saw his jaw relax, his eyes grow soft.

"Close to home?" Hal asked. Blaise nodded.

"Very close. This is my land."

He lifted the reins and the horse moved forward. He turned into the old trail, face lifted to the notch just ahead. Suddenly Hal's eyes narrowed and he leaned out of the saddle, studying the ground.

Riders had recently come this way and there was sign that the trail had been used many times. Hal straightened, aware that Blaise hadn't noticed. He rubbed his thumb along his jaw and then quietly lifted the Colt from the holster, let it drop, making sure it would draw smoothly and swiftly.

They came into the notch. The mountain walls fell away to either side. There were trees in the narrow canyon, big, gnarled oaks that had stood for centuries. Blaise unconsciously quickened his pace, searching ahead along the slope to the left. He glimpsed the house among the trees and his heart lifted. He had come back to a home that he had not seen in a decade. The trail turned and the house and buildings stood in full view. Blaise drew in with a cry of protest.

The place was a ruin. Two small sheds had fallen down. The corral was no more than bare poles sticking up out of the grass-covered ground. A door had fallen from the bunkhouse and there was no glass in the window. The roof sagged.

The main house was in fair condition. It stood solid and square. Blaise saw a rag stuffed into a broken window pane. The yard was knee high in grass and Blaise caught the glint of sun on a tin can. Hal pointed to two saddled horses standing under the big oak.

"You've got visitors."

Blaise hardly heard him. "What have they done to the place?" he demanded. Hal shrugged.

"Ten years, Blaise, and no one to keep it up."

Blaise closed his eyes for a second and then straightened, his shoulders going back, square and firm as his jaw. He spoke quietly to the horse and rode slowly up the path. Hal pulled out a little so that he had a clear view of the door and windows and a greater portion of the yard. The two horses puzzled him.

They came into the shadow of the oak and Blaise reined in. The place looked even more ruinous. He could now see weathered cracks in the door. A few feet away was a small pile of dried garbage; rusted tin cans littered the yard in a wide arc.

The door opened and a man stood framed, hands hooked in his gun belt. A second man appeared and both stepped out into the yard. One was big and fleshy, the other thin, but both had needed a shave for a week. The big man stared boldly at them.

"Strayed, ain't you?" he asked.

"Who are you?" Blaise asked. Hal reined to one side, keeping his eyes on the smaller man, who seemed content to work a cud of tobacco and await developments. The bigger man lifted a brow in surprise.

"Mister, I ask the questions around here. Call your brand or ride off."

"I like to know who visits my place when I'm gone," Blaise said with deadly calm.

The big man turned and looked at the house, the decrepit buildings, as though to make sure. He faced Blaise with a crooked grin.

"You strayed your trail, pilgrim. I'm Gus Peetie, ride for Scorpion. This is part of Scorpion range."

Blaise stiffened and Hal became tense, eyes glued on the smaller man, who had stopped chewing his tobacco. Blaise's hands lay slack on the saddlehorn, but Hal could see the slight movement of a muscle in his jaw.

"Does Leonis claim it?"

"This and the whole range around," Peetie nodded.

Blaise's right hand dropped to his side and his voice became tight. "Then he's a bigger thief than I thought him. I'm Blaise Randell and this is my ranch. Hit your saddles and light out."

They stood glaring at one another. The man's facial muscles hardened, his eyes narrowed. Peetie laughed, an ugly sound.

"When Scorpion takes over a place, it stays. You're bucking a big outfit, Randell. Git while you can."

"Why auger, Peetie?" The second man spoke for the first time.

Blaise's eyes flicked toward him. Peetie's hand jabbed down in a swift, blurring motion. Blaise caught the movement and his own fingers taloned around his gun butt. He sank spurs deep, whirling the horse. Peetie's gun blasted almost before it cleared the holster and the bullet whipped close to Blaise's head. Blaise swiftly lined the Colt and the weapon bucked.

Blaise's slug caught Peetie in the shoulder, spun him half around. The second man had drawn his gun, but Hal's shot whipped his hat from his head. He stood frozen, gun still lifted, hammer dogged back. Hal spoke dryly.

"Just unwrap your fingers, friend, and let her drop. Then step back . . . 'way back, where it's healthy."

The man dropped the gun. Peetie stood holding his shoulder, blood staining his fingers, his heavy face screwed up in pain and anger. Blaise dismounted, picked up the two Colts. Hal chuckled.

"These scorpions done lost their stingers, Blaise. They ain't much good no more."

"By God, you'll be sorry for this!" Peetie blurted.

Blaise didn't answer, but walked to the horses and lifted the rifles from the scabbards. He pitched them to one side. Then he faced the two men.

"Ride out — and don't come back. Tell Leonis that Randell took back what was his and he intends to hold it. If any Scorpion rider comes up this way, he'd better come shooting."

Peetie's glare locked with Blaise, held a moment, then wavered, dropped. He spoke over his shoulder to the second man.

"Come on. We'll be back — and burning powder." He glanced toward the house. "Enjoy it while you can, Randell."

CHAPTER
SEVEN

Blaise watched Peetie and his companion ride down the slope to the trail. Peetie turned and shook his fist. Hal watched, rolling a cigarette. Peetie turned his horse back into the trail and the two men disappeared down the canyon. Blaise watched a moment longer and then slowly turned to survey the house again.

He fought against a combination of circumstances and forces much too great for him. The dirty rag protruding from the window, the deep cracks in the door panels, the scattered cans and rubbish symbolized what time and men had done to him. He had come back filled with dreams. One by one they turned to the laughable vaporings of a fool. From the house he could look back down the canyon between the peaks, and see, at a far distance, a section of the Valley.

It was empty, cattle gone, not even farmed. The drought had killed the cattle, and Leonis had emptied the Valley of Blaise's friends. Melanie had slipped away when he could do nothing but dream between stone walls hundreds of miles to the north. And now his home. He had expected his small stock to be scattered, but he had never foreseen the ruin that time and careless men could bring. He looked bleakly at Hal, who jerked his thumb toward the house.

"We'd better get to work. We can't run cattle with no corrals or barns or fences." He cuffed his hat back from his forehead. "Maybe we'd both better work on the house and then I can rebuild the corral while you start the barn."

His tone was matter of fact, but Blaise still hesitated.

"It'll take a long time. You'd get along better working for someone else."

"Blaise, we throwed in together. This is no fault of yours. I intend to stick around and get some work done. How can we build up a big spread if we're licked before we start?"

He removed the saddles and blankets from the horses and picketed them under the tree. Blaise slowly walked to the door and entered the big main room. Once it had been clean and bright, a cheerful place.

His old table still stood in the center of the room, but it was thick with dirt and scum, scarred by careless spurs or knives. The floor had not been swept in all the time he had been gone, empty bottles and old papers, leaves and dust had gathered in the corners. The windows were dull with dirt and the light in the room was somber. There was no sign of the bright Indian blanket that had once hung on the wall. The fireplace was choked with ashes that had fanned out onto the floor in a cold gray carpet. Streamers of soot hung from the heavy rafters. The chairs were ricketty, one broken. Packing boxes had taken the place of those that were gone.

Blaise felt an inward shudder. He crossed to the bedroom. The door creaked in protest as his push opened it. He faced another dirty window. His old bed was still there but it was covered with a thin and dirty blanket, torn and ragged. The mirror above the washstand was cracked, filthy with fly specks and the top of the stand itself had been scar-burned with countless cigarettes.

Blaise stepped back and slammed shut the door, a seething anger boiling up. He walked to the kitchen. The big range stood rusty and abandoned, Scorpion punchers preferring to cook their meals at the fireplace. But the kitchen was as littered with cans and scraps of refuse as the yard outside. Blaise turned, glad now that he had not seen this when he had driven Peetie and his companion off. There might have been a double killing.

Hal came in, and looked around. For a moment his face grew tight with anger and then it cleared. He spoke impersonally.

"We need a broom and a pail of water. You clean up them windows while I sweep out the place."

Blaise cleaned windows, working fiercely in keeping with his angry mood. Hal swept, raising a cloud of dust, but whistling cheerily. Blaise knew it was for his benefit, but he couldn't lift himself out of his dark anger.

They worked hard and steadily. By dusk they had the main room and the bedroom cleaned so that they were livable. The rag still protruded from the broken window and the soot clung to the rafters but at least the place no longer looked like a pigpen. Hal lit a cigarette, looking around the room with a satisfied air.

"She ain't right yet but we can live, I reckon. Build a fire and I'll bring in the grub."

There was a lamp on the table, only slightly dusty, the bowl filled with oil, and they ate by its light. After the meal Blaise could look around the room with a fair amount of equanimity. Hal lit a cigarette.

"How much range have you got in these mountains?"

"I border the old Encino Rancho to the east," Blaise answered, "about ten miles, I reckon. It goes west beyond Calabasas, if Leonis hasn't fenced it off by now."

"If he has?" Hal asked sharply. Blaise shrugged.

"He'll lose some fence. The ranch is long and narrow, from the edge of the Valley to just below the crest of the mountains on this side. But there's lots of meadows and canyons, plenty of grass. A man needs just enough fence to seal off canyons and meadows."

"That'll mean little riding," Hal nodded.

"Most of it up and down." Blaise arose and stretched. "We'd better hit the blankets. I want to ride early tomorrow to see what needs to be done."

They were riding by sunup. Blaise led the way deeper into the mountains, heading up toward the high ridges. Hal eagerly watched the country. It was, in reality, a maze of canyons and peaks, but he was constantly surprised by the good grass that grew in the canyons that were generally wide, forming small and pleasant meadows. The mountains rose ever higher. Time and again they came on box canyons that needed only a single short length of fence and a gate to make them perfect pastures for a limited number of cattle. It was broken land and, seen from the Valley, almost worthless. But Hal's interest mounted as he saw the possibilities. Blaise felt a rebirth of his hopes.

Twice he came on canyons that had formerly been fenced, but the barriers were gone and hardly any trace remained. But it would take very little to barricade a couple of canyons and bring in a few head of cattle to get started.

Perhaps drought had killed ranching as an important industry south of the Tehachapis, but a limited few could return to it and make money. Leonis was trying it. Blaise's resolve strengthened, and he nearly forgot the anger that had raked him at the first sight of his house. There was far more work than he had expected but he could come out ahead, he saw that clearly.

They were close now to the high ridges and finally Blaise drew rein. He pointed to a distant peak to the west and then toward a high bold rock outcrop to the east.

"I always figured my boundary was on a line between those peaks," he said. "No need to string a fence so I never had the line surveyed."

"Who's your neighbors?"

"Malibu Rancho along part of it, Topanga Rancho and Encino to the east. Good folks, all of 'em, and we never had any trouble."

Hal leaned on the saddle horn. "With this range up here, why did you try homesteading the Valley?"

"I wanted some flat land. I figured I might raise hay and bring in feeders from up north."

"Sounds reasonable."

"Was." Blaise picked up the reins. "But it don't make sense now. Let's head up to the ridgetop."

Blaise came first up on the ridge. The land dropped away below him in a long series of ridges and, afar off, stretched the deep blue of the Pacific, the sun glinting on the ocean waters. Hal came up behind him and suddenly reined in, staring.

"What's that!"

"The ocean."

"I'll be damned!" Hal stared, head moving slowly as he took in the scene from north to south. His voice grew awed. "There can't be that much water in one place."

Blaise grinned and reined the horse around. They dropped below the ridge, Hal still shaking his head. Blaise chuckled now and then. Hal was soon lost again in the maze of canyons, but Blaise led without hesitation, the memory of the country returning without a flaw.

The sun climbed high and they pulled in beneath an oak tree to rest the horses, boil coffee and munch cold biscuits from the saddlebags. They stretched full length in the grass, backs braced by the tree, and lazily surveyed the ridges that marched eastward. Blaise dropped off to sleep.

Only a moment later Blaise's eyes snapped open, some vague warning awakening him. Not thirty feet away a beefy man sat a heavy bay horse. The sun had not tanned his skin, but burned it. He had thick lips, the lower protruding and his washed blue eyes rested steadily on Blaise. Hal grunted and sat up, freezing instantly when he saw the rider. Blaise came to his feet.

"Howdy," Hal said. The rider gave a scant nod.

"Ready to move on now?" he went on. Blaise looked surprised.

"I suppose so. Why?"

"Scorpion rider," Hal said.

"Not me. I'm Faro Raikes, foreman for Thatcher's spread."

"Thatcher?" Blaise asked. "He's new to these parts."

"Rancho de las Montanas," Raikes said and shrugged. "Me, I'd call it something easy like Flying T. But not W.K. with his Eastern ideas of greaser ranchos." He came directly to the point. "Now you've had your sleep, get off our land."

"Your land!" Blaise jerked up his head. "Wait a minute! My boundaries run clean to the Encino grant!"

Raikes eased back in his saddle, shook his head. "Mister, you ain't got any land within half a mile of that oak there. W.K. bought part of the Encino and Malibu grants and some tax land he picked up. No matter, you're on it, and W.K. said to light a fire under trespassers. That means you."

Hal scrambled to his feet as Blaise shook his head stubbornly. "I'm on my own land. If anyone moves off, you do."

Faro looked ugly. "Get off, mister, or get shot."

His hand streaked to his gun. Blaise's Colt blurred, the black muzzle lined down before Raikes could clear his own weapon. The big man sat immobile, frozen.

"Lift it out, easy," Blaise ordered coldly, "and let go."

84

Raikes obeyed, dropping his gun as though it had suddenly grown red hot. Blaise signaled for Hal to pick it up. Raikes scowled.

"You're just asking for trouble, mister. Thatcher don't let no one walk over him."

Hal looked questioningly at Blaise. "Now what?"

"We'll have a talk with this hombre, Thatcher," Blaise said. "I'm tired of having every man I meet claim part of my land."

They mounted and Blaise ordered Raikes to lead the way to his home ranch. Faro looked for a moment as if he wanted to argue, then shrugged and turned his horse to the south. Blaise and Hal fell in behind him, Hal shoving the man's Colt in one of his saddlebags.

Raikes angled through a canyon, led the way over a ridge, into another canyon and onto a trail. It made several looping twists around mountain spurs. Blaise's initial anger passed and he pulled up beside Raikes.

"Who is Thatcher?" he asked.

"A rich gent from the East," Raikes replied readily. "Made shoes back there and sold 'em all over the world, I reckon. He's got more dollars'n the San Fernando's got grass."

"Why'd he come out here?"

"He decided he could let some of his hired hands make shoes for him. He traveled considerable, then landed in California and decided he liked it. He bought himself the ranch, and Thatcher ain't one to do things small. Tried to buy out all of Encino and Malibu, but he only got hunks of 'em. Then he built himself a house."

Raikes paused, awed wonder in his eyes. His voice lowered. "Mister, he just didn't build any old house. He had him some fancy architects and carpenters. He bought wood and glass and stone from all over the damn' country, I reckon. The place has so many rooms down and up, I get lost in it."

Hal's brows rose. "A real big man, huh?"

"They ain't no bigger!" Raikes nodded emphatically. "Why, the bunkhouse is damn' near a mansion and the foreman's house is bigger'n a bank president's. I just can't get comfortable in it. The crew's big enough to work four ranches, but Thatcher wants things that way and he's willing to pay for 'em."

"But he don't get my range," Blaise said tightly.

"We'll see, mister. Thatcher's hard, and what he buys, he keeps."

Raikes would say nothing more. They rode deeper and higher into the hills. Blaise judged they were halfway to the ocean, when Raikes turned along a canyon between two peaks on a course that paralleled the sea.

They came out of the canyon and Blaise suddenly drew rein. Raikes had described the house, but the actual sight of it was a jolting surprise. It stood on a flat-top hill, a veritable castle. It was of brick and timber and Blaise had never seen so many windows. They overlooked the ocean, still some distance away beyond the lower hills.

The higher mountains behind it shielded the house from the northern winds. Just below, stood newly built barns, bunkhouse, cookhouse and outbuildings, seemingly miles of corrals and pens painted a gleaming white. Blaise's eyes widened and he formed a soundless whistle. Raikes grinned, a touch maliciously.

"That's it — Thatcher's play ranch, mister. Think you can buck a man with *dinero* like that?"

Blaise stiffened. "I intend to. Where'll Thatcher be?"

"Up at the house, likely."

"Then ride to the house."

Raikes hooked a leg over the saddlehorn and shook his head. "You don't do it that way on this spread. You get an appointment to see W.K. — or an invitation. You ain't got one."

Blaise laughed. "I've got the best — Judge Colt."

"I got forty men working under me," Raikes said without haste and squinted toward the corrals. "Maybe thirty of 'em is around the place right now. They won't like to see a gun on me, mister. Neither will Thatcher."

Blaise lifted his gun from the holster. "If anyone starts trouble, you'll get the first bullet."

Raikes studied him, shrewdly. Then he put his foot in the stirrup again, picked up the reins. "You're just making it harder."

Blaise signaled him forward. The three riders approached the buildings and were within a few yards of them when a man stepped from the barn. He stood stock still a moment, then wheeled back inside. Raikes spoke over his shoulder.

"The boys don't like it."

"Keep riding," Blaise snapped. "Straight for the house."

The road led past a corral and carriage shed, curved up the slope to make a huge circle before the house. Raikes shrugged patiently and continued riding. Men came out of the barn, stood staring a moment, and then advanced in a body to head off the riders. They spread out in a rough crescent and waited.

They were a varied but competent and clean-cut lot, Blaise saw. One of them stepped forward and raised his hand. He was tall with a rugged, deep-seamed face and steady brown eyes. Raikes pulled in and Blaise halted close behind him.

"What's wrong?" the man asked sharply. "Faro, you need help?"

Raikes sucked in his lips and quizzically raised an eyebrow. "The gent wants to see W. K., Luke."

"But why hold a gun on you, Faro?"

"The gent," Raikes lifted his thumb over his shoulder toward Blaise, "decided it was a quick way to see the Boss."

"Mister, has Faro done you anything wrong?"

"No," Blaise said coldly, "but your boss has stolen some land of mine — claimed he bought it. I aim to see him."

A murmur ran through the men and Luke's face hardened. He seemed to slouch, but Blaise grew more alert, eyes centering on the man. He realized that perhaps he had been a bit headstrong to bring Raikes in like this, but a man had to start to fight sometime. Luke spoke softly.

"Mister, we work for Thatcher, and Las Montanas is our spread. No one calls the Boss a thief or brings in his *segundo* like a roped ridger runner. I reckon you'd better start pulling in your horns."

Blaise sat immovable. Luke waited, his anger slowly overriding his patience. His right hand lifted slightly.

"This is between me and Thatcher," Blaise said. "We can settle it."

"The Boss is from back East," Luke replied levelly. "He's a ring-tailed terror but he probably don't know a butt from a muzzle of a Colt. He ain't no land stealer."

"Who stole land!"

Blaise's head jerked around. The girl had climbed up on the corral and she balanced on the top rail. She dropped to the ground and came striding to the group. Blaise looked more closely. The smoky-blue eyes snapped angrily now. Her hair had a dull coppery glow in the sun. She no longer wore a tailored, costly suit; but jeans, a plaid shirt and small, high-heeled boots.

She came to a halt a few feet away, hands on her slender hips, glaring up at Blaise. "My father never stole anything! And you can —" Recognition dawned. "You! Why you're the man on the stage — !"

Blaise reddened, shoved the gun in the holster and jerked off his hat.

"I — yes, ma'am, it's me." He looked around astounded. "You live here?"

"I'm Rennie Thatcher," she said. Her voice grew sharp. "What's this about Dad stealing land? What's Faro done that you drive him in like a . . . a criminal?"

"Maybe I swung too wide a loop," Blaise answered. He added desperately, "Can I see your dad?"

"You certainly can!" she snapped. Her glance swept the men. "It's all right boys. You'll follow me, Mr . . . ? Mr . . . ?"

"Randell, ma'am, Blaise Randell."

"You can leave your horses at the corral. I'm sure no one will steal them."

Blaise reddened and dismounted. Raikes swung off his horse and pitched the reins to one of the men. Rennie strode away up the road to the big house. Blaise, Hal and Raikes followed her.

The closer they came to the house, the larger it grew. The door was wide, with thick panels that could withstand a battering-ram. Rennie pushed it open and strode inside. A young woman in a black dress and little white cap appeared.

"Where's Father?"

"In the library, mademoiselle."

Blaise gaped but Rennie turned sharply to the left, tapped lightly on a door and pushed it open. The men followed her.

The room was almost as large as Blaise's whole ranch house. One wall was solidly lined with bookshelves, glass enclosed. Another wall was all windows overlooking the distant ocean. The furniture was dark and massive, a heavy table in the center of the room, deep leather chairs placed invitingly. A man arose.

He was portly, but his face was rawboned, strong, the blue eyes imperious. An iron-gray mustache just managed to soften his stern lips. He wore a dressing jacket, and a silk string tie broke the soft white expanse

90

of his shirt. He held a thin cheroot in his lips. A grizzled brow rose when he saw Raikes, then Blaise and Hal.

"What's this?" he demanded. "What is this, Rennie?"

Raikes spoke first, waving a hand toward Blaise and Hal. "I run onto these two on Montanas land, and told 'em to git off."

"He claims," the girl cut in, "that you've stolen land."

"Stolen!" Thatcher's voice lifted and then he grew choleric. "Stolen! Why you young whippersnapper, I never stole a square inch of land from anyone in my life. By Gad, sir, I should have you thrown out of the house!"

"It's still my land, sir," Blaise said stubbornly. "I bought it more'n ten years ago."

Thatcher glared at him and then sensed that Blaise spoke simple truth. He looked at Raikes, Rennie, then sharply back at his foreman.

"Where'd you find him?"

"Ten miles this side of the Encino boundary."

"That, sir, is *my* land," Thatcher snapped.

"It's mine. I bought it fair and square, and I never sold it."

Thatcher grunted angrily. "Wait a minute, young man. I have something to show you."

He strode out of the room. Rennie walked to one of the windows and Blaise covertly watched her. If anything, she was far prettier than she had been on the stagecoach. She must have been thinking of that day, too, for she turned suddenly.

"Did they ever catch the bandits?"

"I don't know. I've been too busy since to find out."

"That was a very brave thing you did — both of you," she stated simply. Blaise made an embarrassed gesture of denial. "But it was. I shan't forget it . . ."

Just then Thatcher came back into the room. He strode to Blaise, who had stood up hastily. Thatcher looked sharply at him and Blaise read the dislike and determination in the man's eyes.

"Your name, sir?" he demanded.

"Blaise Randell."

"I thought so. You've got nerve to come into my house and claim I stole land from you. It's like your kind!"

"Now wait," Blaise cut in, angered, "I don't —"

"*You* wait, sir! You were found guilty of murder and sent to San Quentin. You did own that stretch of land, but it went tax delinquent. It was sold two years ago. I bought it last year."

"Tax delinquent!" Blaise gasped. Thatcher glared at him.

"Exactly. I suppose you had some crooked scheme of frightening me into buying it from you a second time. It won't work, sir. I advise you to forget it."

CHAPTER
EIGHT

"Murderer!" Rennie said in a dismayed, disbelieving voice.

"Exactly that." Thatcher turned. "Tried in Los Angeles . . . and convicted. He would make a wonderful neighbor!"

Blaise pulled himself together. "You've not got the whole story, sir. I've been released and —"

"Verdict reversed?" Thatcher demanded.

"Pardoned."

Thatcher's mustache quivered. "Then California has a very poor governor. I still ask you to get out, sir."

Anger and a blazing sense of injustice blinded Blaise and he felt his whole body shake with a desire to strike Thatcher. Then the room focused again. Rennie stood just beyond Thatcher, her eyes wide with shock. She looked questioningly at Blaise, lifted her hand and let it drop. She turned to the window.

Blaise mastered himself, though he sensed the hopelessness of the situation. "You have a deed to that property?"

"Duly recorded."

"Then I apologize for thinking you stole my land," Blaise said in a strained voice. Thatcher grunted in surprise.

"Accepted, sir, but please leave Las Montanas. We do not welcome murderers."

Blaise jammed his hat on his head. "You will apologize for that someday."

"I doubt it. Good day, sir."

Blaise turned on his heel and strode out of the room, down the hall and outside, Hal following close behind him. Blaise reached the corral, his stride long and angry. Two Montanas punchers silently watched him. He stepped into the saddle, reined the horse around and sank the spurs. The animal shot down the road in a cloud of dust. Hal raced after him.

After a headlong race down a canyon and across a meadow, Blaise's overwhelming anger lessened and he pulled the horse to a walk and then halted to let it blow and rest. He sat dejected, looking up at the rocky crests of the mountains. He could see Thatcher again, face cold and condemning. He saw Rennie's shocked look change to one of certainty and then she had turned her back on him. It had been that, more than all else, that had revealed how thoroughly he must be branded by all who knew of his background.

Hal found him still silently sitting in the saddle, staring morosely at the ground. Hal pulled in beside him. Blaise lifted his head, speaking dully.

"Let's get back to the ranch . . . what's left of it."

"The buzzards sure collected," Hal said shortly and Blaise nodded. He sighed deeply and led the way through the maze of canyons and meadows.

It was nearly dusk when they reached the ranch. Hal unsaddled the horses and turned them into the corral while Blaise went to the house to prepare the evening meal. Hal came in and helped with the work and they sat down to pick over their food, drink deep and often of the coffee and stare glumly at one another.

"How much land did Thatcher get?" Hal asked finally. Blaise jerked out of his dark thoughts.

"It's the land I bought from the old Encino Rancho, maybe a little over half of my graze land. It's got us whipped if all that's gone."

"Thatcher stealing and Leonis ready to fight," Hal shook his head. "Where the hell do you turn?"

"I don't know," Blaise answered. He roused himself and sat forward, leaning his elbows on the table. "But Thatcher didn't steal that land. He bought it fair from someone. Delinquent taxes! What chance did I have to pay them?"

Hal didn't answer. Blaise folded his hands and stared at his thumbs. "We just can't lose everything . . . there's a way out, there has to be!"

"I sure wish I could see it," Hal shook his head. He asked hopefully, "Without that Encino stretch, we'd have enough to get along?"

"This land is mostly straight up and down," Blaise said. "The best meadows and pastures are on the old Encino grant. Together, they'd make a good spread. Separate, they're hunger outfits."

"Taxes," Hal shook his head in disgust. Suddenly he looked up. "Say, if that section was delinquent, what about this one? Maybe Leonis *does* own it!"

Blaise stared at him, jaw dropping. "Lord, I never thought of that."

"Trouble," Hal said bitterly, "is like a stampede. It rolls over you and more keeps a'coming."

Blaise cast over the possibilities and found them dark. It could easily be that he no longer owned a foot of this land and he was a trespasser on his own rancho. The thought was bitter. Melanie gone, land gone, an outcast . . . he wondered why he had ever come back.

Suddenly he lifted his head, listening. Hal still glumly watched the flame in the lamp chimney. Blaise caught the dull thud of a hoof from the corral, the faint sigh of wind in the trees. Then he heard it faintly again. A horse came slowly up the slope from below . . . slowly and quietly. Blaise stood up and blew out the lamp.

"What —" Hal started.

"Visitors," Blaise said sharply.

"Scorpion riders!" Hal breathed.

Blaise crossed the room to the door, partially opened it. His hand slid the Colt out of the holster and his thumb rested on the hammer spur. His eyes strained down the slope into the shadows under the trees. He heard Hal at the window and both men became still, listening.

Then Blaise caught a movement against the dark trees. He lifted his Colt and he heard the click of Hal's weapon as the man dogged back the hammer.

"Blaise! Blaise Randell!" a voice called. Blaise didn't recognize it and Hal's sibilant whisper cut across the darkness.

"Play it careful, *amigo*."

Blaise stepped to one side so that only his head projected beyond the doorframe. He slammed the door back against the wall in a loud crash. He half expected bullets but none came.

"Is that you, Blaise?" the voice called. The shadow moved again, closer, resolving itself into a horse and slender rider.

"Who is it?" Blaise called.

"Me . . . Walt Case. I been lost in these blamed hills since sundown."

Blaise strode out the door, holstering his gun. He reached the boy just as Walt swung out of the saddle. "Is anything wrong at home?"

"Wrong? Not that I heard of."

"Then what are you doing here?"

Walt half turned, one hand still on the saddlehorn. He scuffed at the dirt with his boot, looked up at the white blur of Blaise's face and then away.

"Well . . . I wanted to . . . I reckon I just slipped away and come over here."

Blaise stared at him. Light came on in the house as Hal relit the lamp, and Blaise could see Walt more clearly. He took the horse's reins.

"Well, you're here. Had supper yet?"

"No." Walt strode along beside him to the corral and took off the saddle while Blaise removed the bridle. He dropped the saddle on the ground just outside the gate. "Uh, Blaise, I figured I'd stay awhile."

Blaise grinned in the darkness. "We'll talk about that after you've had some grub."

The boy was hungry and his coming had somehow broken the strangling hold of despair that had ridden Blaise. He found his appetite had returned. As he ate, he asked about Paul Case, Melanie and the others, making certain beyond doubt that nothing was wrong over in the Conejo.

"How did you come?" Blaise asked, pushing the tin plate aside and picking up his coffee cup.

"Over the hill through Calabasas," Walt replied.

"I'd be a little careful of Leonis," Blaise said. Walt grinned.

"He don't scare me none. He's the reason I come."

"Leonis?"

"Sure. You and him'll be fighting, and I ain't too young to help you get started and maybe show Leonis he ain't such a big dog."

"You!" Blaise demanded. Walt nodded eagerly, then caught the note of disbelief in Blaise's voice and flushed. He lowered his eyes and spoke almost sullenly.

"I'm eighteen and fullgrown. It ain't like I couldn't carry my own share. I can ride and I'm strong, though maybe I don't know much about ranching." He looked up, eagerly. "But you and Hal could teach me, and I can handle a gun good. Why, we'd do all right an . . ."

He caught the strange expression on Blaise's face and the words died on his lips. He looked at Hal, who

98

sat slouched back, one brow cocked high, watching Blaise. Walt looked puzzled.

"Something wrong?" he asked, and rushed on, "You think maybe I'm too much of a kid?"

"No," Blaise said softly. "You make a man, Walt. Does Paul know you're here?"

Walt's eyes clouded angrily. "Dad listens too much to Mark Davis. He won't do nothing. He didn't want me to come here. If you was my friend, I'd sure ride out to do what I could."

"You slipped away," Blaise said. Walt nodded, hanging his head. Blaise looked at Hal. This boy had dared trouble at home to offer his services on a ranch that could hardly be said to exist. The irony of the thing struck him and a bubbling laugh came to his lips, a bitter sound that made Walt look up. Hal grinned crookedly, reading Blaise's thoughts.

"It don't make sense, does it?"

"None at all," Blaise agreed. Walt jerked erect, shoving the chair back, face flushed.

"You mean me. You mean I ain't man —"

"We don't mean you," Blaise cut in. He sobered and held out his hand. "Walt, I appreciate having found a friend who'll stand by me. There ain't many of them in these parts."

Walt hesitated, searching his face. Then he grinned and took Blaise's hand, suddenly looking gangly and awkward again.

"Thanks, Blaise. I heard what you done — before. I'm right proud to ride with you now."

Blaise sat down. "Point is, Walt, we just found maybe there ain't no range to ride, at least that belongs to me. Besides, I don't want Paul mad at me because of you."

"I can't stay here?"

"Not right at first," Blaise said, carefully picking his words. He explained about the loss of the Encino section and what might have happened to the rest. "Me and Hal will ride to Los Angeles tomorrow, to see where we stand, or if we can't yet redeem the section we lost. You ride home. If we get things straightened up and need you, we'll send word."

Blaise looked directly at Walt. "The next time you won't slip off. You'll talk it over with Paul like a man. That's the only way, son."

Walt read finality in Blaise's eyes and knew it was useless to argue. Blaise hitched closer to the table, his attention on Hal now.

"We'll ride Walt to the pass and see he's on his way home. Then we'll strike for Los Angeles by way of Gomez Station and the Verdugo Pass. We'll see what the records say."

By dawn the three men saddled up, Walt with no enthusiasm for the job. They rode down the canyon and threaded the hills to the Valley floor. Walt came in close beside Blaise.

"Look, why can't I stay until you get back from Los Angeles? Maybe something'll happen and you'll need someone to look after the place."

"That's exactly why you're not staying," Blaise said in a friendly tone. "Leonis may be on the warpath and I don't know how things will turn out with Thatcher. It

100

could get mighty hot around here and I can't let you get hurt alone. Paul would never forget it and I'd always be blamed. That's how it has to stand."

Walt slumped dejectedly and rode on. They crossed the highway and headed for distant Chatsworth and the mountains. It was still early when they reached the village and started up the winding road into the mountains.

At last they reached the saddle of the pass and reined in. Blaise placed his hand on Walt's shoulder.

"I thank you for riding to help, Walt. But you know how things stand. Tell Paul I said he's got a son he can be proud of."

"Thanks, Blaise," Walt stammered. He looked up swiftly. "You'll sure call me?"

"As soon as we need you," Blaise promised. Walt lifted the reins and rode down the grade toward the distant Simi Valley.

Blaise sighed, partially in relief, and reined his horse back toward the San Fernando. They heard the rattle of chains and the rumble of heavy wheels as a big freight wagon came toiling up toward the pass. Slim Starling handled the reins. Blaise pulled to one side of the road and waited.

Slim reined in on the level stretch and the horses blew loudly. He kicked on the brake and then threw a leg over the edge of the seat. He jerked his thumb over his shoulder toward the high canvas above the wagon bed.

"Flour for Simi and hardware for Fillmore. As soon as I deliver it, I'll be heading your way in a couple or three days."

"Better wait awhile, Slim. We found things badly tangled over there."

"Leonis claiming the rancho?" Slim asked. "You could gamble on that. It'll take more'n you two to keep that old land grabber in his place."

Blaise admitted that Leonis had taken possession, but he told how they had cleared the rancho only to learn of Thatcher's apparently legal claim to a large portion of it. Slim listened, surprised and troubled. At last he picked up the reins.

"Maybe it's just another of Leonis' slick moves," he said hopefully. "It'd be like him to sell another man's land to some fool Easterner that wouldn't know the difference. Looks like you need me more'n ever. I'll sure roll this damn' wagon and get back fast."

"All right, Slim. We'll meet you at the rancho after we come back from Los Angeles. If we get a ranch, we'll work it. If we haven't —" He shrugged eloquently.

"You'll have her." Slim paused, grinned. "Maybe you'll be lucky and Thatcher'll get burned out. There's a helluva fire over in them mountains. I saw it as I started up the grade. See you later."

He kicked off the brake and shouted the horse into motion. The wagon gathered speed on the downgrade and soon disappeared around the bend. Hal watched it and then turned, looking at Blaise.

"For a killer, mister," he said with a grin, "you sure got friends. I wish I had as good back in Arizona. Well, lead the way to Los Angeles."

102

Blaise started at a fast trot down the grade, gradually increasing speed. Hal caught up with him and looked his question. Blaise's eyes were troubled.

"Slim said there was a fire. Could be most anywhere in the mountains, but I'd like to make sure."

They wound through the mountains at a fast pace. They came out on the final ridge and immediately saw the dirty gray cloud high against the southern sky. Hal could see it was a big fire, burning deeper into the distant Santa Monicas toward the ocean. He jerked around when he heard Blaise's exclamation. The man's eyes were wide, his face stricken.

"That's us!"

Blaise grimly raked the spurs and rocketted down the last slope. Hal raced to catch up with him and both rode at breakneck speed through the village and out into the Valley beyond.

Blaise strained to see the distant hills more clearly, trying to determine the point where the fire had begun. Smoke pall hid the higher peaks as the wind whipped the flames up toward the crest.

In that broken country, no one would attempt to check the flames until they threatened some rancho. Otherwise they could ravage miles of sage and hillside until they burned themselves out at the ocean's edge.

As they watched, sudden bright flares and billowing columns of black smoke marked where big clumps of sumac burned fiercely. Over it all was the gray-yellow smoke of the sagebrush, flaming along the mountain slopes. Already he could see the black carpet of ruin the fire left behind it.

They reached the highway, plunged across. Now even Hal could see that their *rancho* was dangerously close to the fire. Blaise raced on, using spurs to speed the horse up the first slopes. They had not yet reached the burned area but it lay ahead of them, a black blight. Blaise could see the flames now, licking along the topmost ridge. They dropped below the far slope and only the rolling, fierce smoke clouds marked the fire's progress into the mountain chain.

Blaise turned into the ranch road, racing up it to the narrow opening of the canyon, through the portal. He reined in, face suddenly white. The ranch house was only smoldering, hot ashes, the chimney standing grim and black above the ruins. Blaise scarcely heard Hal rein in beside him, or the man's amazed oath.

Beyond the ruins of the house the fire had flamed up over the wall of the canyon and then had burst free into the tinder-dry mountain country beyond. The corral was gone. Only the decrepit bunkhouse remained. Blaise looked around with stricken eyes.

Leonis had returned an answer to his challenge.

CHAPTER
NINE

A bright tongue of flame leaped up from the ashes, burned brightly a moment and then snuffed out, leaving only a wisp of smoke. Blaise sat immobile, eyes glassy as he looked from one pile of ashes to another and then up the blackened slope.

"Leonis!" he said in a choked voice. "Leonis!"

"I'm for riding to Calabasas," Hal said, "and cleaning out the place."

Blaise slowly shook his head. "Not yet. Let's look around for sign."

"The fire?" Hal asked indicating the huge column of smoke lifting beyond the ridge. Blaise dismounted.

"No chance of ever stopping it now. It'll burn out and no harm done. There's nothing up in the hills."

"Thatcher's?"

Blaise studied the smoke again and lifted his hand to test the wind. "They'll be all right the way the wind holds. Besides, the fire'd be there and gone by the time we rode in."

Hal squinted up at the smoke and also tested the wind. It blew steadily at an angle that would take it away from the big Montanas Rancho. Satisfied, he dismounted and walked with Blaise to the ashes that marked what once had been the house.

They were still hot. Blaise stared over the expanse a moment, face tight, and then hunted for sign.

The ground held sign, plenty of it, but all of it old. Not only had Blaise and Hal walked back and forth across it, but untold Scorpion riders in the days before Blaise had retaken possession. The hard packed ground yielded nothing definite. Then Hal and Blaise split, each casting out in an ever-increasing circle.

Hal called Blaise to a clump of burned manzanita. He pointed to a charred can, the type used to carry coal-oil. It lay two or three yards within the area of the hot ashes and Blaise could only study it at a distance.

"Maybe," he said. "It was thick with brush before the fire, and the can might've been there a long time without us seeing it."

"And it could've been throwed there just before they struck the match," Hal insisted.

"Sure," Blaise agreed. "Let's look for something more."

They turned back toward that portion of the ranch yard that the flames had missed. Hal searched the corral while Blaise went directly to the bunkhouse. He pushed open the door, saw that the dust on the floor had been undisturbed. He worked down the slope and at last stopped, calling Hal.

"Horses, at least three of them. They stood here while the riders set the fire."

The traces of them were plain. The riders had evidently watched the buildings burn awhile and then, satisfied, had ridden back down the canyon toward the Valley floor.

Hal hitched at his gun belt, looking narrow-eyed down the pass. "That's good enough for me. I'd head for Calabasas."

Blaise stood silent, studying the tracks, then lifted his head and looked back at the smoke, now further away beyond the ridges. He bit his lip.

"Maybe it's good enough for me, and you, Hal, but we need more — a lot more."

"Why, man —"

"Proof for you and me," Blaise cut in swiftly. "But Leonis hog-tied me once before. Maybe he's waiting for us to come riding in to get his hide."

"You're not just sitting your horse like a drunken Indian, are you?" Hal demanded.

"I'm not going scalp-hunting without better proof," Blaise snapped. "Any three riders could've made those tracks, Hal . . . Scorpion riders, pilgrims passing through, maybe some of Vasquez's ridge-runners if they're in the neighborhood — or even Raikes and some Montanas riders. Who were they?"

"Scorpion!" Hal snapped.

"I'd back that bet," Blaise nodded, "But I can't prove it. Leonis could kill us out of hand if we went after him . . . what could we prove outside them tracks? I'll have hard facts before I jump him. I've had enough of guards and cells and stone walls."

Hal grumbled but subsided. He turned back toward the house and distastefully surveyed the ruins.

"So what do we do? Give up?"

"No," Blaise said so sharply that Hal jerked his head around. "We can build a corral and live in the shack. We got the land —"

"If Thatcher'll let you have it," Hal snapped.

"We'll check on that. Maybe it's not gone. Scorpion or Las Montanas won't drive me out."

Hal shrugged disconsolately and pulled a tobacco sack from his shirt pocket. His eyes slowly swept the ruin as he rolled the cigarette, lit it and inhaled deeply.

"I never seen a ranch any flatter'n this one. And what'll be left of the graze after the fire?"

"None . . . where it burns. But grass east and west of us is untouched." Blaise dropped his hand on his friend's shoulder. "I figure we'd still better ride to Los Angeles. After that, we'll see what we can do."

Hal sighed. "There's only one thing left to do . . . unlimber our Colts and collect us some hides until people learn to leave us alone."

Blaise saw no need to reply. They rode grimly out of the canyon and back along the trail that wound down to the Valley. On the spine of the last ridge, Blaise drew rein and his eyes coldly swept over the Valley, coming to rest for a moment on the low ridges that hid Calabasas.

"Looks like no one was interested in the fire," he said evenly. He folded his hands on the saddlehorn and leaned forward on them. "Of course, it was up in the hills and folks let 'em burn out."

"But your rancho's up there. They knew you'd come back."

"They knew I'd come back," Blaise nodded. "Leonis knew it, the Thatchers knew it. No one come."

"They expected it," Hal snapped.

"Or didn't care," Blaise added. "There's always that." He straightened and touched the horse's flanks with his spurs.

They reached the dusty road and turned eastward. For a time Blaise moodily watched the heavy smoke pall that obscured the southern sky. The fire must have burned over a thousand acres by now, and Blaise noticed that the smoke streamed off slightly toward the east and south, the intense heat of the flames having undoubtedly changed the air currents. He thought of the big Thatcher rancho and studied the smoke a little more closely. It would pass Las Montanas slightly to the west, he decided, and the buildings themselves should be in no immediate danger.

Satisfied, Blaise set his face toward Los Angeles. Anger gradually left him, giving way to an ever-increasing mood of despondency. He had the dull, crushed feeling that perhaps he had been a fool and a dreamer all along, that he faced too great a task against too many odds. Even this present journey appeared useless. He would only find more trouble in the distant Pueblo of the Angels.

He sank deeper into his thoughts, picking over the factors arrayed against him one by one, trying honestly to evaluate them and, even more, himself and his chances.

Leonis might no longer be the fighting hellion of ten years before, but he still ruled Calabasas and the Valley from his stronghold on the Scorpion range. Blaise felt sure that Leonis had fired the rancho. It was so like the man of old to destroy what he could not possess.

Melanie had deserted him. Blaise faced the fact squarely now in this moment of defeat. She had left him while he was still locked securely behind thick walls. Blaise's thoughts slowly revolved about her, and her marriage with Mark Davis. It dawned on him that, amazingly enough, he did not feel a deep sense of desolation and loss.

And then, unaccountably, his thoughts swung to Rennie Thatcher. He recalled how she had looked on the stage, a tall and stately girl. He saw her then as she had been at Las Montanas, still tall, now lovely in jeans and shirt.

She had looked so shocked and disbelieving when her father had accused him of being a murderer. And when he did not deny the charge, he could again clearly see the quick flash of emotion, gone in a second, and then detestation. His mind dwelt on that quick succession of expressions. They seemed important, though he inwardly laughed at the thought. She had simply been shocked that a criminal had come into her home. It would happen a hundred times again in his life unless he found who had killed Chavez.

He dwelt on that killing as he rode toward the mountains that cut the Valley from the coastal plain. Chavez had been a sneaking bully, a man who spoke loudly of his own worth, while he ran off a head or two of his neighbor's beef on dark nights. Blaise had lost a couple of steers and had trailed them to Chavez's

110

disreputable *rancheria* in the shadow of the Chatsworth rocks.

He had found the steers, and Chavez, bleating swift and frightened lies, all the bravado gone. Blaise had flattened him a couple of times and then kicked the gun from the man's hand, when Chavez tried to draw and kill him. Blaise had jerked the man to his feet. "You'll draw on the wrong man someday and he'll slap a bullet between your eyes. If I ever catch you anywhere near my range or wearing a gun, you'll be in bed for a month."

He had driven the stolen steers back to his rancho. There had been trouble before with Chavez; Paul Case and the others knew of it. Leonis had undoubtedly known, too.

Blaise's lips curled angrily as he thought how easy it had been for Leonis to move quietly in. He or a Scorpion man had killed Chavez two nights later. The man's gun and belt had been found in Blaise's rancho while he rode the hills. Leonis and some of the Scorpion crew had captured Blaise and taken him directly to Los Angeles and the jail. Paul, Melanie, and the others had testified for him, but the prosecution had used the known facts of the bad blood between Blaise and Chavez, the belt and gun to convince a jury. The judge had given a life sentence. It had been that easy. It had taken ten years, innumerable appeals to the governor, and a great deal of money to get a pardon. But the murder stigma remained and it always would until Blaise found which Scorpion killer had shot Chavez.

Hal broke in on his thoughts. "That fire is still raising hell in the hills."

Blaise half turned and watched the spread of smoke. It dirtied the whole sky to the south. It had burned closer to Las Montanas, but it still looked as though it would pass by at a safe margin.

Blaise faced the road again, the despondent mood lessening. He had a stubborn determination to meet the situation. It had become quite important to erase the expression of disgust he had seen in Rennie Thatcher's eyes, a symbol of the attitude of the whole world. If nothing else, he had to establish his right to meet every man, and woman, squarely and openly.

It was late when they arrived in Los Angeles and all the public offices were closed. So they stayed overnight in a cheap hotel not far from the Plaza, sleeping fitfully, disturbed by the constant noise from the street below.

Sometime late in the night Blaise awoke. The street was unaccountably still except for a single voice singing an old Spanish love song. The singer's steps sounded loud on the wooden planks, his voice clear so that Blaise could hear the words about a beautiful señorita whom the singer loved and for whom he would overcome all obstacles.

The voice slowly faded away down the street. Blaise lay in the darkness, straining to hear the last faint note, feeling a new sense of peace and certainty. He drifted off to quiet sleep.

The next morning Blaise finally located the recorder's map for the Calabasas section, found his rancho on it. But the whole east portion had been broken off and Blaise's lips tightened as he traced the records.

Finally he looked up, turned to stare at Hal, who shook his head, puzzled. Blaise read the record again.

"The taxes went delinquent, and it was bid for purchase. It shows I was served with notice of intent to buy." He looked hard at Hal. "But nothing ever came to the jail . . . nothing."

"Might be easy to get around that," Hal said.

"It was sold for back taxes, and then resold within a month to Thatcher," Blaise continued. His finger stabbed down to a name, pressed hard. "But it wasn't Leonis, Hal. It wasn't him at all."

Hal shook his head. "Why would Mark Davis buy up tax land so close to Scorpion?"

"I don't know, unless it's buy and sell on a quick deal. Thatcher's the one that'd have to fight Leonis. But Mark Davis!"

"And he filed notice to purchase the rest a few days before you came back." Hal studied the book, then looked up at Blaise. "No wonder that jasper didn't want you to go back to ranching. You sure jiggered up his plans."

Blaise signaled a clerk and questioned him about the entries. Within half an hour he had paid all back taxes on the portion left to his title and had filed a notice of intent to redeem on that portion sold to Thatcher.

"You got to pay for all improvements since the sale," the clerk warned, "and you got just a month to redeem. Your time's up then."

"Any way Thatcher can refuse?" Blaise asked.

"None, unless you don't serve him with this notice of intent. He must have bought it from Davis, knowing it was tax land."

Blaise started back to the Valley within half an hour. Both he and Hal were thoughtful and silent, Blaise trying to understand the new development. He couldn't understand Mark's motives for buying up the rancho, picking up land in the San Fernando when all his interests lay across the mountains.

But Blaise had saved his own land and now he tried to plan a short distance into the future. He had very little money left and he would have to use it carefully. He'd go over into Simi or Conejo and buy up a few head of the best cattle he could find. He'd drive them into one of the wider canyon pastures. He and Hal could get along with what was left of the ranch buildings with a little repairs. By next year, they should be showing some progress.

They took Cahuenga Pass through the mountains and rode down into the Valley. There was still smoke far away across the mountains to the south, but so little that Blaise knew it had finally reached the ocean's edge and was burning itself out. The range would remain blackened until the fall and spring rains, and then the grass and sumac would come up again next year.

They approached the stage stop where Vasquez had attempted his holdup and, once again, there was a line of saddled horses before the hitchrack. Blaise and Hal rode up and dismounted, Blaise idly noting there were many brands on the horses. He looped the reins around the rack and strode toward the building.

He was but a few yards from the door when it opened and Faro Raikes stepped out. Blaise halted and Faro stood immobile with surprise. Then, without warning, his lips curled in a snarl and his hand streaked for his gun.

Blaise acted instinctively. He threw himself to one side, his hand plunging down to his holster. Raikes's bullet sang close and then Blaise's Colt dropped and lined. Raikes looked into the black muzzle and froze, his own gun half lifted for the second shot.

Hal ducked under the rail, gun in his hand, staring in surprise at Raikes and Blaise. Thatcher and Rennie appeared behind Raikes.

Rennie's eyes widened when she saw Blaise, then narrowed in blazing anger. She pushed aside the foreman and came striding angrily to Blaise, completely ignoring the gun. She stopped within a foot of him, regarding him with a contempt as stinging as a whip.

Abruptly her palm slapped solidly against Blaise's cheek. It caught him off balance and the force of the blow jerked his head to one side.

Instantly Raikes's gun hand jerked but Hal snapped, "Don't try it, Faro. You won't live to finish it."

Rennie stood tall and straight. "I wish I were a man," she said in a quivering voice. "I wish I could meet you on equal terms."

Blaise stared at her, his hand against his cheek. Thatcher made sputtering sounds behind Raikes, who stood blocking the doorway, afraid to move against the threat of Hal's gun.

"What did I do?" Blaise finally caught his voice.

115

"What did you do!" she said in acid scorn. She pointed toward the distant smoke. "I suppose you know nothing about that!"

"Sure, but —"

"Oh, you admit it! Murder isn't enough for you. Now you try to burn us alive because we bought land you let slip out of your fingers!"

"I burn you out!" Blaise was thunderstruck.

Thatcher finally shoved Raikes aside and came storming out to Blaise. His shaggy brows knotted down and his lips quivered. He shook his fist in Blaise's face.

"You won't get away with this, believe me! As soon as I reach a sheriff in Los Angeles, you'll be back behind bars. Arson will put you away where you won't endanger anyone else."

"But I didn't set the fire!" Blaise dropped his Colt back in the holster and held out his hands in unconscious appeal. "I had nothing to do with it."

Rennie tossed her head, voice sharp and cutting. "Lies! See what good it does you before a judge . . . if you haven't run out of the country before the sheriff comes for you. Come on, Dad."

She turned and strode to the hitchrack. Thatcher glared at Blaise, then followed her. He ordered Raikes to saddle. The foreman eyed Hal's leveled weapon, licked his lips. Slowly and carefully, he lowered his own Colt and placed it in the holster. He came down the steps, crossed the yard and swung into the saddle.

Blaise took a step forward. Rennie lifted her quirt from the saddlehorn. "I'll use this," she warned, and sharply reined her horse around, setting the spurs. It

116

shot out of the yard and up the road. Thatcher and Raikes were left behind, but they jerked their horses around and raced after her.

Raikes turned and shook his fist. Hal slowly holstered his gun.

"Arson!" He faced Blaise. "You said once this was sudden country. I believe you."

CHAPTER
TEN

Blaise ran for his horse, snatched free the reins and vaulted into the saddle. The horse bolted in a swift race after the others. Hal yelled something that Blaise did not hear.

He saw Rennie pull in her horse as Thatcher and Raikes caught up with her. A moment later, they heard Blaise's thundering approach. Raikes jerked around in startled anger. He pulled his gun and, in a swift chopping motion, brought it down and fired.

Blaise heard the whine of the bullet but he kept on, making no attempt to draw his own weapon. Raikes lifted the gun again and fired, the bullet kicking up dust just ahead. Blaise didn't swerve. He saw Rennie rein against Raikes and grab his wrist as he raised the gun a third time. The foreman argued with her and then Blaise pulled his horse to a sliding halt beside them. Rennie swung herself in between Raikes and Blaise.

"You can't stop us," she said.

"I'm not trying," Blaise snapped. "I just ask you to listen."

"To a murderer!" Thatcher demanded. "An arsonist!"

Blaise twisted around. "Don't you believe in two sides to a story?"

Thatcher settled to the saddle. "All right, have your say."

"It'll be lies," Rennie cut in.

"You, too?" Blaise looked at her. She flushed. Raikes leveled his gun.

"Let me blow him out of the saddle," he asked. Thatcher shook his head.

"We'll listen. Then we'll let the law do our work for us."

All three of them looked at Blaise, faces cold, eyes suspicious. He could feel their hatred. He took a deep breath, and told how he and Hal had first seen the fire on the far side of the Valley, and of the destruction done by the time they reached the ranch.

"It was ahead of us then, over a couple of ridges and racing like a stampede. We could never have worked around ahead of it. It was burning straight south and looked like it would miss your place by miles."

"Your place set afire?" Rennie asked in disbelief.

"Who'd do it?" Thatcher asked scornfully.

"We thought maybe you'd done it," Blaise said. "You don't want to lose that land of mine you'd bought. I sure couldn't bother you if I was burned out and had to leave."

"Why that's the most crazy, ridiculous thing I ever heard!" Rennie exclaimed.

"Is it?" Blaise demanded. "Raikes or some of your men might've done it on orders. It's no crazier than you getting an arson warrant on me." Blaise smiled tightly. "At least I waited until I could get a chance to find out. That's more'n you've done."

She met his gaze squarely. A dull red crept up her neck and into her cheeks. She studied her hands. Thatcher cleared his throat.

"You've got proof?"

"Ride to my spread and see," Blaise offered. Thatcher slapped his thigh.

"All right, we will. Maybe we've been hasty." He drew himself up. "I'm not a man to be walked on, sir, but I do think I'm just and fair. If you're right, you'll have my apologies."

"Thanks," Blaise nodded, adding cynically, "not that it rebuilds the ranch or proves that you didn't order the fire set and it got out of hand."

"You have our word for that!" Rennie's head jerked up, her eyes flashing. Blaise considered her levelly.

"As you had mine back there at the station." He shrugged. "But I keep forgetting I'm a criminal."

He reined around. She made a gesture of protest that Blaise did not see. She glanced at her father, who only shrugged and turned to follow Blaise back to the station.

Hal had waited, watching closely for the first sign of trouble. Now he trotted easily forward, reined around and fell in beside Blaise. He spoke low.

"You could've been blowed right out of the saddle."

Blaise grinned. "I never thought of it. I had to prove to them I didn't set the fire."

"Them?" Hal asked softly. "Or her?"

"Them!" Blaise repeated emphatically and a moment later wondered if he was so certain. He shrugged off the ridiculous thought.

120

They rode at a fast pace. Blaise and Hal in front, the Thatchers and Raikes following. They reached the ranch road and Blaise led the way deep into the hills, finally climbing up to his canyon and drawing rein before the remains of the house.

Thatcher and Rennie looked around, missing none of the destruction. Finally Thatcher dismounted. Blaise led him to the bushes where the burned oil can lay. Thatcher studied it as Rennie came up the slope to them. She stopped before Blaise.

"We wronged you. I'm sorry."

"I apologize, too, Mr. Randell," Thatcher said quietly. "We might have made a bad mistake. But why would Leonis want to do this?"

Blaise explained the use to which Leonis had put the ranch during the prison years.

Thatcher scratched his chin and looked up the slope where the fire had sped. Rennie watched Blaise closely, then asked directly and bluntly, "And did you murder a man?"

"No."

"Rennie," Thatcher cut in, "I think I need a talk with Mr. Randell. Could you come with us to Las Montanas, sir?" He smiled wryly. "You will not be ordered out again."

"I could. Why?"

Thatcher's jaw grew hard. "I think I'm going to take a hand in the local situation. I'd like to hear more of your story before I decide which side I will join."

Thatcher and Rennie wanted to ride directly through the canyons to their ranch, but Blaise knew that the fire had left a hock-deep layer of black ash, some of it still smoldering. So they took the long way about by the roads.

Just at twilight they came to the meadow and ridge on which the ranch stood. Blaise saw how close Las Montanas had come to destruction. The fire had jumped a neighboring ridge, and a cross wind had whipped it at a sharp angle directly at the ranch buildings. Two smaller structures had been burned, and black ash marked the fire's progress up the ridge toward the giant main house. But it had been beaten off and had swept on to the distant ocean.

"You had a hot fight," Blaise said. Thatcher nodded grimly.

"Very hot. We thought it was all going. It will ruin everything for years to come."

"Next year, after the rains, the grass will grow," Blaise assured him. "I've seen it happen before."

The servant met them at the door. Thatcher had them shown to a bedroom as large as the bunkhouse back at the ranch, the windows overlooking the blackened canyons to the south and west. Hal gently tested the bed after the servant left and looked around at the rich wallpaper, the thick drapes at the windows, the heavy dresser and chairs.

"My blood ain't going to take this, partner. How could one man get so much money?"

"Not ranching in these parts," Blaise answered and sat down wearily. A breeze came in the window, bringing the scent of burned wood and brush. He looked around the room. "Leonis would be against someone bigger'n him, if Thatcher took a hand on our side."

"It's about time that someone give us a hand," Hal said dryly and dropped on the bed.

Just before dusk a servant came in and lit the lamps, two more brought water for baths. Within an hour another servant announced dinner.

The dining room was long and high, the table the largest Blaise had ever seen. He had never been served before and he felt nervous and out of place. Hal was more openly uncomfortable. Both men were glad when the ordeal was over, and Thatcher led the way to the big library where he gave them cigars and waved them to easy chairs. Rennie followed them.

"This concerns all of us," she told her father. He shrugged and said nothing more. He pulled up a chair and lit his own cigar, then looked at Blaise.

"I've heard something about you, Randell. There's been some talk of you in Chatsworth and Calabasas. It made you an undesirable neighbor."

"Leonis in Calabasas," Blaise said, "maybe some of his friends in Chatsworth."

"Mmm," Thatcher growled. "Maybe we'd better have your side of the story. Got any proof for it?"

"All the people in Conejo Valley," Blaise said, "who've known me for years. My own word, for the time when Chavez was shot."

"Character proof only," Thatcher said and studied the end of his cigar. "Sometimes that's enough. I'll listen."

Blaise told the story of his quarrel with Chavez, of the trouble with Leonis and the raids in the Valley and how he had tried to fight back and have his friends stand firm for their own rights. Then he told of the killing, the sudden arrest, trial and his sentence to San Quentin and the years he spent there.

He finished and, for a time, there was silence in the room. Thatcher sat in a brown study. Rennie had edged to the front of her chair and she watched Blaise, eyes wide with understanding and compassion. Blaise caught her look and it hit him hard, surprisingly so. His eyes moved swiftly away. Thatcher stirred.

"Pardoned, and it took years. It took money, too?"

"All I had, practically," Blaise nodded. "I'd had some good years before Leonis pinned the Chavez murder on me. He didn't want anyone taking up land in the Valley."

"The land, you say, was open to homestead. How could Leonis keep anyone from filing?"

"He couldn't," Blaise answered swiftly, "but he could give them so much trouble that they'd never last long enough to prove up. Leonis had some of his riders file and then he planned to buy from them when they had full title. But that's long and slow, and others came in . . . my friends in the Valley and I filed down there. Leonis always figured the land should have been his."

Thatcher looked toward Rennie to note her reaction. His eyes widened and he looked sharply back at Blaise, then his glance shot to Hal.

"And Mr. King? He's never been fully explained."

124

"My friend," Blaise said simply. Thatcher's eyes warmed slightly.

"In the West a sufficient explanation," he agreed. "But I'm from the East, and we haven't been that generous in a couple of generations that I know of."

"Your bad luck," Blaise said with a grin. He sobered. "Hal and me are together, trying to build up the rancho."

"Tell the rest, Blaise," Hal cut in dryly. "I served a term for robbery. I don't want to go back with the old bunch that tangled me up before. Blaise asked me to throw in with him. I accepted."

"Guilty?" Thatcher asked abruptly.

"Of making a fool mistake and running with the wrong crowd. I learned my lesson. It's a fresh start down here."

"Thanks to Mr. Randell," Rennie said softly. Hal turned to her, and smiled as he nodded.

"Thanks to Blaise," he agreed.

Thatcher leaned forward and slapped his hands on his knees. "It sounds like a straight story, Randell. My daughter has told me how you handled the outlaws who tried to rob the stage. That's in your favor. Now, you think Leonis set the fire?"

"I'm certain of it."

"It threatened us," Thatcher said slowly. "If Leonis is land hungry, then he'll probably attack Las Montanas once he's driven you off and made sure of the Valley."

"Maybe," Blaise said dubiously. "The drought hit him hard and he's lost a lot of beef . . . land hunger with it."

"Market's picking up," Thatcher said shortly. "It won't support big ranchos like the old days, but it will pay a few to go back to cattle. It's Leonis' chance. Yours, too, and Leonis will know it. He'll try to knock you out again."

Thatcher puffed on the cigar and considered the far wall. "That's exactly the way he'll figure. He could dominate the beef market in Los Angeles. He could move in on Las Montanas then, and we'd have damn' near a losing fight."

Blaise had a growing admiration for the old man. Thatcher might be from the East and not too familiar with cattle, but his forecast seemed accurate. Thatcher leaned forward.

"All right, Randell, I'll go the whole way. I propose you and I work together to fight Leonis. Between us, we should be able to hold him off. Agreed?"

"I'd like to, sir," Blaise said slowly, "but I have to tell you something else."

Thatcher's eyes narrowed, but he said nothing, waiting. Blaise looked embarrassed but determined.

"I checked on the sale of my land to you by tax title. I still have a month in which to redeem. I'm giving you notice that I will."

Thatcher laughed, a relieved sound. "Randell, I want that section, but I guess it belongs to you. I'll accept the redemption payment and deed it back. It's your legal right. But that has nothing to do with Leonis."

Blaise sighed gustily and grinned. "I figured you might give me a fight about that land."

126

Thatcher drummed his fingers on the chair arm, judging Blaise, studying him from head to foot, stroking his mustache slowly. At last he dropped his palm on the chair arm.

"I make quick decisions, Randell. I've had to in my business. You're a case in point."

"Me?"

"You've two jobs to do. You must clear yourself of that Chavez business . . . that's your problem. You've Leonis to keep in bounds . . . I can help you there. But once the situation is such that you can ranch without danger of raids or burnings, and once you're cleared of murder, I'll back you financially in cattle raising."

"Back me!" Blaise jerked erect. Thatcher nodded and pointed his cigar at Blaise.

"I think you're worth the gamble. But you've got a job before I'd advance you a cent. Otherwise, it would be damned bad business, and no one has ever yet justly called me a fool."

Thatcher felt that they had covered the pressing questions and he suggested that Rennie play for them. They went into another room where she played the piano for nearly an hour, singing now and then in a sultry voice.

Blaise listened, amazed and entranced. He was not quite sure how it happened, but soon after he strolled with her along the edge of the ridge before the house. The moon rode high, lighting the peaks and throwing a silvery pathway across the dark expanse of the distant ocean. The stars were full and bright, numerous beyond counting, and the night wind was gentle with just a touch of chill.

They walked slowly to the far edge of the yard. Rennie halted facing the ocean, head back, breathing deeply. Blaise stood close by, watching her, aware of some new, magnetic quality about this beautiful girl. She spoke in a half whisper.

"It's lovely . . . all this."

"Yes," he said and something in his voice brought her around, startled.

They stood close, looking at one another. Blaise did not realize that he moved, but she was even closer, and his head bent down. He kissed her. She stood quiet, lips soft against his. Her fingers pressed deep into his arms a moment and then she hastily stepped back.

Her eyes were wide and wondering, lips parted. Blaise waited, breathless. He could feel the tingle of her lips even yet, the pressure of her fingers on his arms.

"I . . . Oh, Blaise, you shouldn't!"

She ran to the house. Blaise watched her go, heard the door close. He took a deep breath and turned to face the ocean again, the bright moon-path that glittered and pulsated now.

For this moment, at least, the world had become beautiful and wonderful again.

CHAPTER
ELEVEN

Early the next morning, Rennie wished them good luck and it seemed to Blaise that her voice held a deep and personal meaning.

"You clear up the Chavez matter," she said, her eyes meeting his. "It is important."

"I'll do what I can."

"You'll have to do more than that, Mr. Randell."

Blaise and Hal walked down to the corral. While they saddled their horses, Raikes climbed to a seat on the top rail. Blaise immediately walked over to the fence, extending his hand.

"No hard feelings, Faro? You started shooting before I knew what it was all about."

Faro dropped to the ground, and accepted Blaise's hand, "None . . . except you're mighty fast. Next time, I'll keep my hand plumb away from my Colt."

They rode away from Las Montanas. Blaise looked back, half hoping for a glimpse of Rennie, but she had evidently remained in the house. He faced the trail again, wondering why he felt so disappointed. He thought of last night and the kiss, the way she had studied him afterward and then fled. He thought of all the wealth of Las Montanas, a symbol of the greater wealth of Thatcher himself.

He grinned wryly, wondering and questioning. A criminal, a shoe-string rancher on the edge of ruin . . . that was Blaise Randell, who had kissed an heiress and now had the unutterable gall to read subtle meaning into no more than friendly advice.

Suddenly Melanie came to his mind; fair, golden Melanie, who had been his dream for so many years, who had been vital and alive and then suddenly beyond his reach, Mark Davis's wife. He could see her face clearly. He soberly wondered why Rennie seemed so important now, close on the heels of his loss of Melanie. Did the loss of the one, throw him headlong toward the other? The thought troubled him, until he saw the situation impersonally again. Melanie was of the past, gone. Rennie was not even of the present, or the future . . . she was unattainable.

Blaise cut off the main trail and took the direct route to his own rancho. It led through the heart of the burned land and black ash rolled up in choking clouds. Blaise pulled his neckerchief up over his mouth and nose, his hat brim low. Even so, the fine ash penetrated the cloth and made breathing difficult. Charred limbs of sumac left black, sooty marks along their levis. Now and then they had to turn aside to avoid still hot patches of smoldering ash.

They saved miles, but it was with a feeling of relief that Blaise topped the last ridge and looked down the blackened slope to his ranch. He instantly saw the saddled horse, ground hitched by the bunkhouse door.

"Visitor," he said, jerking down the neckerchief. Hal grinned.

"You look like you're wearing a black mask. Maybe if we just ride in, you'll scare him off."

"You're no beauty yourself." He sobered, inclining his head toward the saddled horse. "No telling who it is."

Hal fell in behind Blaise as they worked down the slope. They passed the charred remains of the house and had just reined in when the bunkhouse door opened and Slim Starling stepped out. His jaw dropped when he saw Blaise and Hal.

"What in hell has happened?"

Hal eased back in the saddle and his hand dropped away from his gun. Blaise made ineffectual attempts to brush the ash from his clothes and then straightened.

"The fire you saw across the Valley started here."

"Deliberate?" Slim asked. Blaise nodded. "Scorpion?"

"We think so."

Slim looked around at the destruction and his jaw hardened by degrees. He cursed softly.

"The jasper who did it ought to be burned himself!"

"We'll get around to it," Blaise said. "But first we've got this place to straighten up."

They picketed the horses and started to work. By high noon, the building was at least livable and clean. Slim cooked dinner and they ate it in the shadow of the bunkhouse. Finished, they rolled cigarettes and leaned back against the wall. They could look down through the canyon notch and see a thin slice of the Valley afar off.

"You going to stay on here, Blaise?"

"Running never did a man any good, Slim. He runs once, he runs again."

"Scorpion won't like it. They could try to burn what they missed this time."

"I have to take the chance. But I'm staying. I'm stocking my range. It'll take gunhawks to haul me off . . . feet first."

Slim looked reflectively toward the Valley. "Leonis has done that before, though no one could prove it."

"Chavez?" Blaise asked swiftly.

"Not him, though I've had ideas about the deal." He sighed. "Lot of people have tried to stand up against Leonis, even before you come to San Fernando, Blaise. Some of 'em ain't been found yet. You be damned careful."

Blaise stretched out his long legs. "I've got two jobs — just two. I'm going to ranch and I'm going to find out who killed Chavez."

Slim idly picked at the wild-oat stubble along the foundation wall. He spoke without looking up. "One's hard enough with Leonis against you. Whyn't you forget the other? It'll be a cold, cold trail."

"I can't," Blaise said simply. Slim looked down toward the Valley.

"Right out there's where my land used to be, up against the Oat Hills this side of the Santa Susanna."

"It was good land, Slim. Paul Case was next to you, his section going up into the rocks."

"Good land," Slim nodded. "Sometimes I wonder if I could get it back again. Not alone. But now you're back and there's some I know over in Conejo who'd have the nerve to buck Leonis. If we worked together, maybe we could swing it this time."

Blaise considered, his face slowly lighting, but he held his voice level. "Sure of those over in Conejo?"

"They've talked, and some I know real well."

"Maybe it could be done." Blaise added a warning. "But cattle's mostly done for."

"Sure, but it could be farmed, or sold at a good price once it was proved up. It never mattered much to me what I did . . . cattle, freighting . . ."

Blaise stirred. "We've done what we can here, Slim, until I can get lumber and material to rebuild. Why don't you ride over to Simi and Conejo and see what your friends think about it?"

Slim scratched his ear. "Need help against Leonis?" he asked.

Blaise laughed. "Plenty of it, and I need good neighbors."

"I believe I will! Won't hurt nothing. I'll ride out come morning."

"No hurry," Blaise said. After a moment's silence, he asked, "What do you know about Mark Davis, Slim?"

Slim looked hard at Blaise, then shrugged and studied the distant Valley again. "You knew him, Blaise."

"Ten years ago. What about now?"

"Oh, about the same. He'd rather make ten dollars tomorrow swinging a close deal than a man-sized dollar today where he stood up and was counted."

"Is he buying up land?"

"He's a farmer!" Slim said flatly and Blaise let the matter drop.

The three men worked hard until dark forced them into the house, where they lit the lamp and cooked supper. They rolled into the rebuilt bunks soon after. Hal and Slim dropped off into sleep almost immediately.

But Blaise lay staring at the dark gray square that marked the window. If new homesteaders came into the Valley, men with courage and determination, then Leonis could be held to his present bounds. With the help of the homesteaders and Thatcher, Blaise could begin to ranch with a good chance of establishing himself. There remained only Chavez's killer, but Blaise felt sure that time often worked for the patient man.

The next morning Slim saddled up right after breakfast. He mounted, held the horse in. "I'll see how many I can get. Not all the boys'll be scared of their shadows. We'll ride over as soon as I get 'em together."

"Better go direct to Los Angeles," Blaise suggested. "File from government maps before Leonis can block you."

Slim considered and nodded. "Watch for us in the Valley."

He lifted his hand and let the impatient horse move off down the canyon. Blaise turned back to the house where Hal leaned in the doorway. He watched Slim ride down the slope and finally drop from sight beyond the canyon.

"Slim's boys," he said. "Las Montanas, you and me. It's stacking up against Scorpion."

"It's time," Blaise said grimly. "We'll ride to Calabasas tomorrow; we've got to get more supplies."

Hal's brows shot up. "Looking for trouble?"

"Not exactly, but we won't run off if it comes. Calabasas is the closest town to get lumber and materials and other supplies. I also want Leonis to know we're still around."

The town looked sleepy and quiet as they rode in. Two men sat on the canopied store porch, chairs back, heels hooked on the rail. But their chairs came down with a thud and they stared as Blaise rode up to the shade of the big oak and hitched his horse to the rail.

"Howdy," he said easily. "Seen Leonis around?"

They shook their heads almost in unison, and then one caught his speech. "He ain't been round for nigh a week . . . out to the ranch, I reckon."

"A week," Blaise said. "About the time of the fire up in the hills."

He mounted the low steps to the porch, the men slowly turning to face him. Hal slouched against the oak, watchfully rolling a cigarette. Blaise crossed the porch and walked into the store.

The aproned owner stood by as a customer inspected a rifle. Both men looked up, surprise blanking their faces. Blaise looked closely at the man with the rifle, his right hand resting lightly on his hip above his holster. The man hastily shoved the weapon at the storekeeper.

"I — un, I'll — maybe buy it later."

He moved swiftly down the aisle and hastened outside. The storekeeper slowly and gingerly placed the rifle in the rack.

"Bullets," Blaise said. "Forty-five caliber."

"You're Randell?"

"That's right. The bullets?"

The man licked his lips and looked toward the door. He shook his head. "I can't sell 'em to you."

Blaise's jaw tightened. He shoved his hand in his pocket and pulled out a gold coin, dropping it on the counter. The storekeeper's eyes followed his hand, rested on the coin a second and then lifted to Blaise.

"I can't sell nothing to you, Randell. Leonis would drive me out of town."

Blaise stepped close. "I'm buying, no matter what Leonis said. Do I get them?"

The man hastily placed the boxes on the counter. Blaise broke one open and placed a single cartridge by the man's hand.

"Give that to Leonis. Tell him there's more waiting for his ranch-burning scum."

"You — you won't get away with it, Randell." He lifted his hand, palm out. "Look, I'm peaceful, but this town is run by Scorpion."

"I sure feel sorry for you," Blaise said, mocking. "If any of you had stood up ten-fifteen years ago, Leonis would leave the town alone."

Blaise turned on his heel and strode out the door. Hal remained by the tree, perfectly at ease. Three men stood on the porch, afraid to move. Blaise looked them over, contemptuously.

"Scorpion riders?" he asked. All three shook their heads. Blaise grunted. "Same breed of rat then."

He stepped off the porch and joined Hal, passing him some of the cartridges. Hal spoke in a low tone, laughter in his voice.

"I ain't made a move except to smoke a cigarette. But look at them three frozen statues!" He sobered. "Blaise, the town was expecting us."

Blaise led the way to the lumberyard. The dealer acted as frightened and reluctant as the storekeeper. He didn't want to sell on the plea he did not have boards the right length.

"Cut 'em," Blaise snapped. "Hal, you get a wagon and haul it to the ranch. I'm riding to Conejo."

"Why Conejo?" Hal asked.

"I'd like to throw a question or two at Mark Davis. You can take care of things here?"

"Sure," Hal said, "at least all I've seen so far."

Blaise walked out to his horse and mounted, aware of curious eyes. He wheeled the horse and rode slowly and jauntily the length of the street, leaving the town by the west side. He was in Scorpion territory proper now.

However, he rode through the pass and on into the Conejo Valley, meeting only the Buenaventura stage. Once in the Conejo, he rode more easily.

He turned off the main road and soon came in sight of Mark Davis's house. Blaise searched the yard and surrounding fields while yet some distance away, but Mark was not in sight.

Blaise was reluctant to stop at the house if the man was not at home. As he came closer, he could see no sign of life, so he squared his shoulders and rode on by.

He did not like the thought af facing Melanie again. It would probably always be a strain.

Walt and Paul worked a field close to the road. Paul smiled in warm welcome. Walt gave a half-hearted grin. Blaise dismounted and lit a cigarette.

"What brings you over?" Paul asked.

"I want to spot a few head of breed stock," Blaise answered easily.

"You must be getting along," Paul said. "Let's git to the house. Maybe Maw'll have something to eat."

"Has Leonis bothered you?" Walt asked eagerly.

"Some," Blaise acknowledged.

Maw welcomed Blaise with a hug and a kiss. She put coffee and pie on the table. They had just settled when Melanie appeared in the door. She showed surprise when she saw Blaise but he recognized it as an act. He concealed his own uneasiness.

She talked of household chores, but it was no more than a meaningless nervous chatter. Several times Blaise caught her watching him, closely, her eyes troubled. She had seen him pass the house and now she had come here.

Paul brought up the matter of Leonis again. "So Scorpion has left you alone?"

"Hardly," Blaise laughed shortly. He told of the eviction of Scorpion riders, the fire, about Thatcher and the new alliance. They all listened, Walt eagerly, Melanie with growing shadows in her eyes.

"So there's been trouble," Blaise ended, "but it piles up against Leonis. Slim is up in Simi right now, getting together some men who've wanted to homestead."

Paul shook his head. "It'll mean more war in the San Fernando. Scorpion will try to hold the Valley."

"I expect it," Blaise shrugged.

"You'll be sent back to prison!" Melanie exclaimed in a frightened voice. Blaise turned, looking at her in some surprise.

"Not this time. I didn't come back just to be a monkey on a stick for Leonis."

He veered the conversation to cattle. He learned of two or three places where he might find what he wanted, then Paul and Walt had to return to the fields for the afternoon's work. They shook hands with Blaise but Walt lingered.

"You promised I could help."

"I don't need you yet. You help Paul . . . he needs you more."

Blaise walked with them into the yard. Paul had a moment alone with him while Walt went into the barn.

"Maw and me was worried when Walt rode off, Blaise. But you sent him back and you have our thanks."

"None needed, Paul. He'll run into his first trouble quick enough without me dragging him in."

Paul nodded and when Walt reappeared, said goodbye again and walked off to the fields with his son. Blaise watched them for a moment, turned and pulled up short. Melanie stood just behind him.

Her face was drawn, eyes fearful. Blaise took off his hat, waited. She was golden and lovely as ever, but now the sight of her did not produce the old excitement.

Blaise found himself comparing her to Rennie and it confused him. Melanie spoke uncertainly.

"Blaise, you might get hurt or killed, or maybe back in jail."

"I don't think so." He looked sharply at her, Mark Davis's wife. He could not help the touch of bitterness that crept into his voice. "I'll not harm you or yours."

"I know . . . but I worry about you." She looked out across the fields and her voice dropped almost to a whisper. "I've made a mistake, Blaise. I know that now."

"Mistake?"

"I married Mark Davis. It's all wrong. He's not at all like you. Oh, perhaps I shouldn't talk about it, but . . . you should know. It's only fair."

Blaise worked at his hat brim. At last he looked up at her. "It's late, Melanie, much too late."

"I know," she answered with a sigh. "I'll bide by my bargain, but I want to . . . help you all I can, to get established again, clear your name so that I can be proud of you —" She added with a bitter smile, "Even at a distance. Maybe I'd feel as though I'd made up for my mistake in a way."

Blaise felt his heart leap. She said in effect that she loved him and the old emotions, the old dreams swept over him. He met her eyes and she read his thoughts. Hope slowly lighted her eyes and then she saw the shadow pass across his face, the slight tightening of the corners of his lips. He tried to find words. Neither of them saw the buggy coming down the road.

140

"I — thank you, Melanie," Blaise said with difficulty. "It's — something to know. But I ride one trail, you another. That's all either of us can do."

"All?" she asked and then her voice became dull. "You're right, Blaise. Maybe if things had been different —"

"Sure," he said, and tried to lighten his tone. "You were always one to ride the river with, Mel. You're still a friend."

They jerked around when the buggy rattled into the yard. Mark Davis reined in and sat looking at them, something hard and suspicious in his eyes.

"You're back," Melanie said. He nodded, watching Blaise.

"Too early?"

"Why, no," Melanie said. Blaise beat back the inclination to jerk Mark out of the buggy. "Blaise has been telling *all* of us the news. Leonis set fire to his ranch."

Mark's brow lifted in mock surprise. "You came over to hear about it, I suppose?"

"Of course, shouldn't I?" she demanded.

"Get in. We'll go home."

Melanie rebelliously walked around the buggy and climbed into the seat beside him. Mark remained unmoving.

"I just come from Simi," he said. "Cut my business short. There's been a murder!"

"Murder!" Melanie exclaimed. "Who?"

"He was shot in the back — bushwhack. You knew him, Blaise . . . Slim Starling."

CHAPTER
TWELVE

Blaise flinched. Mark challengingly met his stare. Blaise caught his voice.

"Who?"

Mark lifted his hand in an enigmatic gesture. "Everyone in Simi asked that question. They sent for the sheriff at Buenaventura."

"But why?" Blaise demanded.

Mark lifted the reins, rubbed his tongue around inside of his cheek. "They've tried to guess that, too. He had enemies . . . Slim was always fast with his fists." He tightened the reins. "Anything more?"

Blaise looked blankly at him, started to shake his head, and then changed his mind.

"Yes, a question. Maybe we'd better walk over to the barn."

Melanie's eyes widened, misinterpreting Blaise; her hand lifted to her lips. "Blaise! Wait!"

Mark looked around at her and his smile faded. He frowned, indecisive. He licked his lips.

"Ask it here."

Blaise hesitated, then thought that sooner or later Melanie must learn of it. "I found part of my land had gone for taxes. It had been sold to a man named Thatcher."

"So what has that to do with me?" Mark asked but there was an edge of wariness in his voice.

"I rode to the recorder's office. You'd bid it in and sold it to Thatcher. I thought you wanted no land over there."

Mark hesitated, then took a bold front. "I have a right to bid in tax land."

"Sure," Blaise agreed. "But did you buy up other property that belonged to friends of yours?"

"You never told me about this, Mark," Melanie said. Mark made an impatient gesture and lifted the reins.

"It's my business," he said coldly. He slapped the reins and the buggy rolled in a wide circle out the gate to the road. Dust streamed from its wheels as the horse trotted swiftly toward the distant house.

Blaise watched. Mark had told nothing, explained nothing. Blaise turned on his heel and strode swiftly to his horse. He wanted to get to Simi right away. Murder always had a reason behind it.

In the meantime Hal wandered impatiently around the small lumberyard. There was a good deal of cutting to be done and the lumberman apparently intended to take his own time about it. Hal smoked a cigarette, ground it out and asked where he could hire a wagon and a team.

"Bledsaw's, if he'll hire it to you," the lumberman growled.

"He will," Hal grinned.

Hal wandered out to the street. He saw the livery sign and he walked slowly in that direction, right hand never far from his Colt. The town looked sleepy and peaceful again, but like Blaise, Hal could sense eyes watching him. He wondered if someone hadn't already ridden to Scorpion with word that Blaise had dared to come into the town.

After some argument, he hired the wagon and team. Hal drove the rig to the lumberyard and walked out to the street again.

Some horsemen had come in, he could see the saddled mounts lining the saloon hitchrack. They might be Scorpion riders, but Hal dismissed that idea. Scorpion would be scouring the town for Blaise, not lining a bar. Hal squinted up at the sun. He'd give the lumberman another hour to load up the wagon.

He walked leisurely to the saloon. He mounted the steps, pushed open the door and entered, alert, eyes jumping from the two men at the bar to the rest of the empty room. The two glanced over their shoulder and then gave their attention to their whisky. They wore worn holsters, their clothing was nondescript and dusty, faces stubbled with beards. Riders for a small, poor ranch in the neighborhood, Hal decided. He walked up to the bar and ordered.

He took this one fast, ordered a second and stood toying with it, studying the bright labels on the bottles stacked before the mirror. He caught a quick glance from one of the two men, a steady, searching look that any stranger might give another. Hal gave it no particular attention.

His thoughts wandered to Blaise. He remembered how he had first met Blaise in the yard of the prison and he had been strangely drawn to the tall man. Hal had been embittered then, planning his revenge on a society that had turned a drunken, thoughtless prank into five long years of prison.

Something of his hatred had shown in his eyes and finally in his speech. Blaise had managed, in the few short minutes alotted them, gradually to redirect his hate and finally show it to Hal for what it was — worthless and a potential breeder of many more years in prison. It had taken months but finally Hal had seen the point.

In time, by the use of devious prison means, they had become cellmates and Hal had learned the story behind Blaise's imprisonment. His own bitterness, in comparison, had its roots in an insignificant incident. But Blaise had always been hopeful. Hal had learned of his past, his plans for the future. He had known Melanie long years before he had met her.

As he thought of the girl, he rubbed his hand along his jaw sensing an inward restlessness. She was everything that Blaise had said — and more. He remembered how he had caught his breath when he had first seen her and how, during the ride to the Case farm, he had tried not to stare in open admiration. He understood why Blaise had dreamed of her.

But she had failed Blaise. Hal could not understand it but, strangely, it gave him hope. Blaise had given her up, Hal could tell it by his actions and talk. Perhaps

145

Rennie Thatcher had something to do with it, another beautiful woman but with none of Melanie's appeal.

". . . burned half the mountains," the voice intruded on Hal's thoughts. One of the strangers spoke to the barkeep. "We was over looking at it. Bad blaze."

Hal, interested, watched the men in the mirror. One of them tossed down his drink. "It was bad, all right. Burned like hell."

"Took one ranch," the other man said, "Damn' near burned it all down. Who owned it?"

"It's a line camp now," the bartender said, "part of the Scorpion spread."

Hal straightened. "It was a line camp, mister."

"Your place?" one of the men asked quickly.

"Me and my partner's. We drove off a couple of Scorpion gunhawks." Hal looked squarely at the barkeep. "You wouldn't know how it started?"

"Not anyhow!" the bartender disclaimed hurriedly. "I just saw her burn, that's all."

"No Scorpion riders was up that way?"

The bartender leaned forward. "Mister, my trade comes from Scorpion, and I stay in this town because Leonis lets me. I ain't saying riders went up there or they didn't."

Hal studied him, then grinned and shoved his glass forward. "Fill it and have one yourself. No harm asking."

"No — but maybe plenty in telling." He filled Hal's glass and walked down the bar. One of the men hitched up his gun belt and walked out the door.

146

Silence settled on the room again. Hal glanced over his shoulder at the yellow-faced clock and settled himself more comfortably. The man returned, walked to the bar and took the drink he ordered to a table a few feet away.

Two more men came in, duplicates of the first pair. They gave Hal a sharp glance and joined the man at the bar. Hal looked at the clock again, decided it was about time to return to the lumberyard. One of the two who had just come in, walked to the poker table, spoke a brief word and returned to the bar, to Hal's right.

Hal flipped down his drink and spun a coin along the zinc to the bartender. He turned to leave and then sank back against the bar, suddenly alert. The four had changed positions. A man stood to either side. The man at the poker table faced Hal, his drink untouched before him. The fourth man lounged against the doorframe, watching Hal closely.

Hal sensed gun-trap. He stood dead-center of the four, a target that one of them would be bound to hit. The bartender had not noticed the setup, but busied himself polishing a glass. Hal's glance moved to each, read the unmistakeable signs in the set of a jaw, a narrowed eye, lips slightly pressed. They wanted his scalp.

They waited, confident, Hal could start things when he wanted to, they left it up to him. He leaned lazily against the bar, considering the situation. If he turned to either man at the bar, he could be taken from behind. If he walked to the door, the three stood at his rear, and he had no chance. The man at the table was just as bad, for Hal would still have three behind him.

Hal straightened easily and instantly he saw the four men stiffen. He turned and asked the bartender for a bottle. He picked it up, examined the label and then slowly walked with it to the table. The man blinked, confused by the unexpected move.

"I reckon we're both strangers to these parts," Hal said with a careless grin and thudded the bottle on the tabletop. "So how about a drink?"

"Drink?" the man stammered.

"Sure, why not? It's a good brand. Here, see the label."

He held the bottle forward with his left hand, half circling the table. The man shot a questioning glance at his friends and then looked down at the bottle.

Hal's hand streaked to his hip and the Colt blurred up. The muzzle bored deep in the man's stomach, the hammer dogging back with a loud click. Hal spoke quietly.

"You're very dead, friend, if one of your pals tries a bushwhack. I'm bound to pull the trigger, no matter where a slug hits me."

The man's hand had involuntarily jerked toward his own holster, but it froze, held out at an awkward angle, the fingers widespread. He sucked in his breath, gulped, eyes wide in panic.

The others had drawn their guns and three black muzzles threatened Hal. But they didn't fire; their grim-set faces slowly changed as they looked questioningly at one another.

148

"I don't savvy why you picked on me," Hal said, "but I never did like a cold deck. You by the door, move to one side."

"You go to hell!" the man spat explosively but a swift warning from one of the others checked him.

"You wanta kill Joe?"

"Do you?" Hal asked with a taunting grin. The man at the door scowled, but he didn't move. The man at the far end of the bar edged around so that he came in Hal's line of vision, gun still leveled.

"Joe won't like a slug in his stomach," Hal warned. He saw a door at the rear of the room that might lead to the alley. He lifted Joe's Colt from the holster and jerked his head toward the door. "We take a walk."

"Go to hell!" Joe snapped.

"I probably will, you with me," Hal agreed. "But first we walk."

"Make me," Joe said with sudden courage. Hal dared not to shoot him, for then his protection was gone. Joe would stand right where he was.

Hal's smile became fixed as he saw the impasse. Sooner or later he would have to make a break, and then the other three would have him.

The door opened and a fifth man strode in. He was tall and dark with a wisp of a mustache, raffishly handsome. Hal instantly recognized the man who had tried to hold up the stagecoach. These were not Scorpion riders!

"What is it!" the newcomer demanded. The man at the door made a slight motion toward Hal with his Colt.

"He has Joe dead to rights. We wing him, Joe gets a slug in his belly."

"He means it, Tiburicio," the man at the far end of the bar warned.

Joe's eyes fastened on the newcomer. Hope showed in his face. The newcomer stood weighing the situation. He smiled crookedly at Hal.

"You think fast, *amigo*. My boys are not always caught so neatly." He looked at the man by the door. "Is he the one?"

"It's him."

The newcomer moved further into the room. "We have gone to your ranch, *señor*. Unfortunately you were not there."

"You're Vasquez? What would you want with Blaise and me?" Hal asked.

"To persuade you to leave, *señor*. You are not wanted."

Hal studied him, keeping the gun muzzle pressed tightly in Joe's stomach. "Now why would a *bandido* care if we stay up in the hills? Or maybe Leonis hired you."

Hal caught the slight flicker in the man's eyes. He'd guessed wrong, it wasn't Leonis. Vasquez shrugged elaborately.

"*Quien sabe?* Who knows?"

Joe tried to shrink away from the gun but Hal kept it close against him. Vasquez moved farther into the room, smiling. He slowly lowered his hand, lifted his gun from the holster. Joe's eyes widened and the sweat popped out on his forehead.

150

"Tiburicio! He'll kill me, sure!"

"It's too big a chance!" the man at the door warned.

Vasquez's brow lifted. Hal watched. He dared not swing his gun from Joe if Vasquez decided on a shoot-out. The bandit bluffed . . . he wouldn't endanger one of his own men. Vasquez held the gun at his side, muzzle lifted. His lips parted in a wider grin and then suddenly his teeth clenched, the muscles around his mouth hardening.

At the same instant he fired. A mighty, invisible sledge struck Hal's arm, knocking up the gun even as galvanized muscles spasmodically pulled the trigger. The bullet ripped up through Joe's throat and out the back of his head. The man fell, dead before he hit the floor. Hal's fingers loosened and the gun dropped.

He stared at Vasquez, face wreathed in gunsmoke that slowly dissipated. The others stood thunderstruck, watching their leader, forgetting Hal altogether. The man by the door licked his dry lips.

"It killed him!"

"Joe always make trouble," Vasquez said, "always grumble. He would have died sooner or later." He nodded toward Hal. "Rope him and bring him along. Señor Leonis may come."

The three men stood stone silent and Vasquez frowned. Only then did they close in on Hal, helpless with a useless, bleeding arm.

CHAPTER
THIRTEEN

Blaise rode grimly into Simi. The day was clear and bright with woolly white clouds high in the jewel-like sky. Simi huddled in the valley, basking in the sun, peaceful and serene. Blaise dismounted before the boxlike undertaking parlor.

He opened the door and stepped inside. The dark drapes were tired and dusty, the carpeting faded, there was an odor of flowers kept long over their time.

A man opened a door in the rear of the hall and came forward. He smelled of chemicals. He had yellow teeth and a sallow skin. He spoke in a low tone, his voice deep with unctuous sorrow.

"A man was shot," Blaise answered his question. "Slim Starling. I want to see him."

"Not yet," the man sadly shook his head. "He is not prepared."

"He was my friend." Blaise said shortly. "I want to see how he was killed."

"But . . ." The man took another look at Blaise's set face. He lifted his shoulders in a resigned gesture. "He's back here."

Blaise followed the man into the bare workroom. Slim lay on a table and Blaise slowly approached. After a second, he said, "Turn him over."

The bullet hole was plain between the shoulder blades to one side of the spine. Blaise studied it, lifted his eyes to the undertaker.

"Forty-five slug."

"At fairly close range. He probably never knew what hit him." He licked his lips. "A friend of yours?"

"Good friend."

"He had others," the undertaker sighed. "Some of them are in town now — at Grogan's Saloon, I believe. They — ah, contributed toward the funeral expenses."

Blaise left the parlor, glad to breathe clean air again. As he walked to the saloon, a hard anger gripped him. Slim had died without even knowing that an enemy was close. Blaise recalled the old days when Scorpion raiders struck out of the night without warning. This killing bore the same trademark.

He found five glum men lined up at the bar. Blaise ordered a drink, carefully watched the men through the bar mirror. Each man in his way gave Blaise a favorable impression. The nearest one suddenly banged his shot glass on the bar top.

"Hell, I can't help thinking about Slim!" he growled. He sighed. "You still can't figure he's dead!"

Blaise half turned. "Who shot him?"

The man looked up, blue eyes turning hard. The others craned to see Blaise.

"Did you know Slim?" the man asked.

"He left my rancho in the Santa Monicas to come over here."

"You must be Blaise Randell." The man shoved out his hand. "I'm Charlie Stivers."

The others pressed around, introducing themselves. There was lanky Bill Denver and a rawhide oldster named Ed Tolliver; a young man, lean as a rail with hawklike eyes, named George Uhl. The fifth man was fat with a moon face and a lazy drawl, Ike Allen. They threw swift questions at Blaise, who walked to a big poker table and sat down, the five men circling it.

"Maybe we'd better compare trail sign," Blaise said. "I heard about Slim this morning and rode over from Conejo. I just saw him."

"Murdered," Stivers said tightly. "Shot in the back."

"When? And who?"

Allen mopped the sweat from his fleshy face. "Mister, if we knew, there'd be a hanging in five minutes. It happened last night. Slim come in yesterday morning and rode around to see all of us."

Blaise eyes circled them. "You all live here?"

Young Uhl shoved his hands deep in his pockets. "I live in town. The rest work at ranches round-about. Slim did a heap of riding yesterday. He told each of us something about his idea and we was to meet here last night to talk it over."

Bill Denver spat elaborately to one side. "We was all here, waiting for Slim. There was a shot toward the edge of town. George went outside but couldn't see nothing and come back in. We had a drink and then

154

some gent rushed in saying a man had been shot. It was Slim."

"Nothing else?" Blaise asked. Stivers shook his head.

"Nothing. A Mexican thought he heard someone running off, that's all." He looked straight at Blaise. "Slim said he was backing your play against Leonis. It wasn't clear. Maybe you'd better tell us."

Blaise told them about the old days, and how Slim had been one of those Leonis had driven off. He spoke of the new battle that shaped up between himself and Scorpion, how Slim had wanted to take a hand.

"That's about it," he finished. "Slim hated to see all that empty Valley. He thought of you boys, said you'd buck the devil himself for land like that. You're farmers, he said, but you want a chance for land of your own. It's out there."

Allen sat down in a chair that creaked in protest to his weight. His bland face was in sharp contrast to the hard, angry gleam in his eyes.

"Maybe you got an idea who killed Slim?"

Blaise shook his head. "I'm just guessing strong."

"Leonis," Allen nodded. Blaise lifted his hand in a slight gesture but the fat man shook his head. "Sure, you don't know. Neither do we, for a fact. But I figure to stake some San Fernando land, hoping Scorpion don't like it. How about you fellows?"

He looked around. The four nodded. Blaise looked from one man to the other, searching.

"You're asking for bullets. Slim would've told you that."

"Slim's dead," Ed Tolliver said slowly, "and we don't like it. If Scorpion did it, then Scorpion asked for trouble. Besides, we'd like some government land."

"All right," Blaise said finally. "Ride with me and look over the Valley. Make your choice and file homestead before Leonis knows anything about it. I'll help you — you help me."

"Sounds neighborly," Tolliver agreed, "seeing you and Scorpion don't get along much. I'll ride."

"Me, too," Uhl snapped and the rest agreed. Slim would be buried early the next morning and all of them would go directly from the funeral to Blaise's rancho.

It was midmorning before they were able to ride to San Fernando, but they set a steady pace that soon brought them to the mountains and through the pass to the wider Valley beyond. As they came down out of the hills above Chatsworth, Allen looked out over the sun-drenched land below.

"It's good. No wonder Slim always said he'd be coming back here someday."

"Good land," Blaise nodded and added, "maybe fighting land."

"When wasn't it always so?" Tolliver asked.

They rode slowly across the Valley. They came to the first ridges of the Santa Monicas and Blaise reined in so that they could see the spread of the Valley below them. They sat silent for a long time, looking, studying. Then Tolliver nodded.

"Gives a man an idea what he wants. We can sort of divide it up when we get to the rancho."

156

They rode through the notch and up to the ranch. Blaise looked for the pile of lumber, didn't see it, then he noticed that Hal's horse was not in the corral. He dismounted, worried, and walked with quick strides to the bunkhouse. A glance told him Hal had not spent the night. Blaise stepped outside, looked swiftly around for further sign.

"Something wrong?" Allen asked.

"My partner's not here. He was to bring lumber back. He's not returned from Calabasas."

"Scorpion's town!"

"The nearest place for lumber," Blaise said shortly. Tolliver leaned forward, his leathery jaw moving in a slow rhythm on a tobacco cud.

"Maybe we'd better look-see."

"I'll go myself," Blaise said shortly. Uhl pushed his horse forward.

"Like hell! We just left Slim, remember?"

Blaise swung into the saddle and grimly reined around. There was a hail from the top of the hill and Blaise twisted about, looking up.

Rennie Thatcher sat her horse on the ridge, a beautiful picture against the sky. She waved and then moved down the slope, letting the horse pick its way among the ashes and boulders. Young Uhl whistled soundlessly.

"Hey, we should've come over sooner! Who's she?"

Blaise explained swiftly and then rode out to meet her. She smiled at him and looked a question at the five men, who watched her with varying degrees of interest.

"New friends," Blaise said, and told of Slim's death and why the five men had returned with him. Her eyes widened.

"You think Leonis did it?"

"Who else?" he asked impatiently.

"I don't know. How would Leonis know where to ambush him?"

Blaise stared at her, realizing that she was right. He lifted his hat and scratched his head, considering the whole circumstance again. He saw he had simply jumped to the conclusion that Leonis or a Scorpion rider had done the killing.

"But — who else would want to kill him?"

Rennie shook her head. "I know so little about all of this. Maybe if you and Hal . . . where is he?"

"I don't know. I left him getting lumber in Calabasas. There was a chance he rode over to Las Montanas."

"I haven't seen him."

Blaise's lips set. "If something's happened, I'll *know* who to blame this time. We're going to Calabasas."

"I'll ride with you."

"You will not!" he exclaimed sharply and then caught himself. His voice lowered. "I'd feel mighty bad if something happened to you."

She looked up at him, her violet eyes suddenly questioning and soft. Blaise's face grew warm. She smiled.

"I'll ride and tell Dad. You might need help."

She turned her horse and, with a last smile, set it at the slope. Blaise watched her climb to the ridge. He slowly reined his horse and returned to the men. Uhl watched the ridge where Rennie had disappeared, his young face bemused. He glanced at Blaise, envious. He sighed, a long and windy sound.

"Blaise, you're sure lucky. Wish I had a neighbor like her. And the way she smiled!"

"Let's ride to Calabasas," Blaise growled, face fiery red. Allen chuckled as Blaise set spurs and streaked down the slope to the canyon entrance.

They were ready for trouble when they rode into Calabasas, though it looked peaceful and sleepy. Blaise narrowly watched the windows and doors as they entered the town, riding directly to the lumberyard. The men behind him spread out, alert and ready.

Blaise turned into the gate. He saw a single stack of lumber ready for loading in the center of the yard, but there was no one around. He dismounted and the five men turned their horses so that they faced the entrance.

Blaise strode across the yard to the little office shack, jerked open the door. The owner sat at his desk. He looked at Blaise with dislike. Blaise closed the door and leaned against it.

"Where's my friend?"

The man stirred slightly. "I don't know. He went to the saloon, there was shooting."

Blaise's eyes grew bleak. "Then what?"

"They rode your friend out of town . . . the last we saw of him. I left the lumber stacked."

"Scorpion?" Blaise asked.

"I never saw 'em. Some say they wasn't."

"I think they lied," Blaise said evenly. The man lifted his shoulders.

"That's your guess. Me, I don't know." Blaise turned to the door and the man added hastily. "What about that lumber?"

"I got more'n wood on my mind."

Blaise closed the door and walked to his horse. Allen gave him a questioning glance. "Saloon," Blaise said. "There was a gun fight."

"Dead?"

"Don't know. But God pity Leonis if he is."

Blaise led the way out of the yard. As they came out on the street, loafers at the store ducked back inside. Blaise reined in before the saloon and this time the five men walked in behind him. The bartender's hand dropped below the bar, but Blaise's Colt blurred out.

"Keep 'em where we can see 'em. It's healthier."

The bartender hastily jerked his hands back up on the zinc. Blaise came slowly to the bar.

"There was a shooting here," he said coldly. "Tell me about it and tell the truth."

"Sure . . . sure, all I can. What you want to know?"

"I hear my friend was in the ruckus, and they took him out of town."

The bartender nodded and described the swift attack. "We buried the man your friend shot the next morning. No one knowed him."

"A new Scorpion rider?"

"No, we didn't know any of 'em, but one . . . Vasquez."

"Vasquez?" Blaise demanded, surprised. He finally shook his head. "The story won't stick, friend."

"Blaise," Allen said suddenly, "customer's coming in."

The batwings burst open and Hercule Leonis stepped in. Three of his riders pressed close behind him. Leonis saw Blaise and stopped short, his eyes swinging to the other five. His heavy lips set and Blaise could see the steel come into his eyes. Perhaps it was the way the light struck his face, but Leonis looked older, tired. His gaze turned back to Blaise.

"I told you never to come back to this town," he said heavily.

Blaise answered evenly, closely watching the big man. "You didn't expect me, Leonis, after you trapped my friend and rode him off?"

"Friend? Trapped! What are you talking about?"

"Quit bucking," Blaise snapped. "What did your hired *bandidos* do with Hal King?"

Leonis stared at Blaise. "Randell, I have no love for you, and I would not like your friends. But I hired no one to set a trap for him . . . or you. I, Hercule, would do it myself and not use others." He looked beyond Blaise's shoulder at the bartender. "What is this, Hank?"

The bartender told him. Leonis' brows drew down in a deep frown and his big hand slowly closed into a fist.

"*Tonnerre!*" Leonis roared. "Tiburicio Vasquez! He dares me! He slaps at my face! I have sent word that he would die if he came to Scorpion or this town! You are certain, Hank?"

"They took this gent's friend off after Vasquez shot him through the arm. They cut for the hills to the south."

"Vasquez!" Leonis turned on his heel to the man directly behind him. "Double our riders on the south range."

Blaise stood puzzled, uncertain. The big man's anger was open and honest. Leonis glared at Blaise.

"You come to help your friend, eh? I can understand that. Now you learn that I have not done this thing. You will leave town then in peace. You have a reason to come. I respect it."

Blaise spoke carefully. "Did you know Slim Starling?"

Leonis cocked his big head to one side. "I do not know him."

Blaise tried another angle. "Were any of your boys over in Simi?"

Leonis answered impatiently. "Certainly not! I have nothing in that valley, nothing that I want. Scorpion is enough. Why do you ask?"

"Slim was murdered . . . shot in the back. Hal King was trapped and some riders took him off."

Leonis studied Blaise, considering the information. "It is easy to see why you blame me, after what has happened between us in the past. But I have nothing to do with either. I do not know your Slim Starling. Vasquez kidnapped your Hal King. I shall settle with Vasquez, because he has come here where I have forbidden."

He turned to leave but Blaise halted him. "Something else, Leonis. You may as well know. A change is coming to the Valley. It won't be like the old days — yours because you had the guns and riders to hold it. Honest men want honest land. They intend to get it. The Valley will be settled and developed."

Leonis' lips curled. "It is strange that a murderer should talk of honest men."

Blaise looked steadily at him. "You should know who killed Chavez."

Leonis laughed. "I know nothing! You could have killed any man and I would have done as I did. You kept those others fighting me, and I saw the chance to send you away for good. It could have been anybody you killed."

His blazing eyes swept the five men at the bar. "These are your friends, men who want to take Valley land. You think you bring new enemies for me. That is your mistake, Randell. I do not care, like in the past. The drought taught me much. Scorpion is large enough with beef prices as they are, and this will never be big cattle country again. Let your friends settle. You look somewhere else for your land grabber, your killer, your kidnapper. It is not Hercule Leonis."

He jabbed his thick, blunt finger at Blaise's chest. "But I also warn you. You have always been a brave man, but a hotheaded, foolish one. In the old days I hated you. Now you are only a trouble, trying to start old fights again. You want war. *Eh bien*, you push me, I give it. Come to Calabasas on business, I do not mind. But come with five men ready to shoot and kill again, that I will not take. You do it once more, I meet you with bullets . . . not words."

He turned and pushed open the batwings with his big shoulders. He stood a moment, half in and half out of the door. His voice became grave, almost courteous.

"There it is between us, do as you will."

CHAPTER
FOURTEEN

The batwings whispered back and forth, and Allen expelled his breath loudly. Tolliver rasped his stubble with his thumb, his eyes distant. Uhl made an impatient sound that stirred Blaise. He turned slowly to the bar.

"A drink," he said. The five joined him.

Blaise toyed with the glass. Leonis had spoken the bare truth. One or two things stood out undeniably. Leonis apparently had not known, nor cared, who had killed Chavez. It had been only the means of getting Blaise permanently out of the old fight. Yet just a moment ago Leonis had made a direct turn-about from all that had motivated him in the past. Anyone could have Valley land, Leonis no longer cared.

Blaise rubbed his hand over his face as though he could clear away his confusion. He faced two problems now, one pressing and immediate. If Scorpion had not killed Slim Starling, who had? If Scorpion had not trapped Hal King, who had? Blaise must shape the question of the old killing in the same manner. If Leonis had not killed Chavez, who had? Who profited? Then and now?

Allen sighed. "That old buzzard was telling the truth, Blaise. What do we do now?"

Blaise lifted his head. "I brought you on a wrong trail."

"Slim?" Allen asked. "Someone killed him, we can still look for the gent. But your partner?"

"I don't know," Blaise replied slowly. "I'll find him."

"We'll help," Uhl offered. Blaise shook his head.

"You'd help more at the ranch right now. Take the lumber back and wait a day or two for me. Uhl, could you ride to Las Montanas so Thatcher won't send men down here looking for trouble?"

The youngster nodded. Tolliver asked, "But what'll you be doing?"

"If Vasquez took Hal, he's got him in some hideout. He'll be looking for riders, a bunch of 'em. One man would have a better chance to scout the country. If I find the hideout, I'll come back for you. If I don't, well, only one of us will have wasted time hunting."

There was some argument, but it was finally settled that way. Blaise hired a team and wagon that Uhl drove to the lumberyard. Blaise gave careful directions to Rancho Las Montanas, then watched the five men ride out of town.

Blaise returned to the saloon and, after he ordered another drink, questioned the barkeeper. He had a rather vague description of the men who had ridden off with Hal.

"Where would Vasquez take a prisoner?" Blaise asked.

"Who'd know?" the barkeeper answered. "His hideout, I reckon."

"It'd be close. Any idea?"

"Just talk . . . and guesses. I've heard it's beyond the pass and into the hills to the southwest. Some say it's a hidden valley. I don't know."

"Over the pass and southwest," Blaise said thoughtfully. "Into the Conejo?"

"From what I hear, right on the south edge."

Blaise bought a few supplies from the store, thrust them in a sack and tied them in the roll behind the saddle. He rode out of Calabasas, climbing the pass to the west.

He knew that Vasquez would have cut south of the highway soon after leaving the town, plunging into the broken hills and canyons. Blaise watched for trail sign but none appeared until he had climbed through the saddle of the pass and had started down into the valley.

He found trace of several horses cutting away to the road toward the south. They could have been made by a Scorpion crew, or by Vasquez. He studied the jumble of hills and rough mountain peaks flung against the southern sky. A man could spend days and weeks in those hills, looking for a particular canyon or valley.

Blaise's lips set and he turned off the road, following the tracks. They followed the curve of the lower hills for several miles, skirting the fringes of the valley. Then they suddenly turned sharply and led Blaise into a cleft between two low hills, circling the base of one and plunging into a narrow canyon that writhed deeper into the mountains.

Blaise rode with mounting hope. No honest working crew would take this torturous way. The tracks entered a rocky canyon and disappeared. Blaise followed along, knowing no rider could scale the sheer walls, certain that he would find the tracks somewhere beyond. But the canyon opened into a narrow grassy meadow, bounded by a rocky stream bed. There were two canyons leading out of it and in the mouth of neither one could Blaise find any sign.

He reined in and settled back in the saddle, reaching for tobacco and cigarettes. He smoked thoughtfully, twisting once to study the meadow, the brush-covered slopes that tilted upward at steep angles. He squinted at the sun, trying to pinpoint himself in this mountain chain. He was south of Conejo and north of the ocean, he could do no better than that.

Blaise chose the canyon before him and rode for a good two miles only to find himself facing a wall of rock. He turned back.

He returned to the meadow and chose the other canyon. He closely watched the ground as he rode along, but there was no sign of a trail. Yet the canyon led on, fairly wide and open. It was the only way the bandits could have gone.

But night caught him in another open glade interspersed with live oaks. The canyon walls were dark with dusk, and high above a single star shone brightly. Blaise reluctantly dismounted and made camp under a tree.

After he had cooked a meager supper over a small fire, he extinguished the flames and placed his saddle under the tree. He lit a cigarette and watched distant moonglow light the sky. It grew brighter until every rock and tree stood out with startling clarity, though the shadows were as black as darkest midnight.

He mulled over Hal's kidnapping and what Leonis had said. He still felt a remnant of doubt. He pulled deep and slow on the cigarette. Finally Blaise shook his head. The more he reviewed the situation, the more it seemed that only Leonis had anything to gain by murder, arson and kidnapping. Blaise finally retrieved his blanket from the roll and curled up in the shadow of the live oak.

He was awake before dawn and had finished his coffee before the sun came up. He saddled, mounted and crossed the meadow, finding a continuation of the canyon on the far side.

It took him a couple of miles deeper and then Blaise faced four or five possible trails. He pulled in, looked carefully around. A quail called cheerily from somewhere in the brush; high overhead a crow circled in lazy spirals. The horse stomped, shook its head. There was no other sound. Blaise settled into the saddle, staring dully before him. Vasquez might be miles away, or just beyond the next jagged peak, down the next winding canyon. Blaise felt anger and futility, a sense of defeat that he wouldn't quite acknowledge.

He picked one of the canyons at random and set his horse into it. It pinched in, huge rock walls hanging silently and ominously over him. Finally Blaise came onto another meadow that sloped upward to a transverse ridge. He set the horse at the slope and drew rein at the top.

He saw that he had almost threaded the mountain range. He could see the ocean, very close now, only three lower ranges intervening between himself and the narrow beach. The range stretched to either side as far as he could see.

Blaise admitted defeat. An army of men could comb this range between the Hueneme sands and the Los Angeles River a month and still miss many hidden valleys and meadows. He could only wait, hoping that he would get some word of Hal.

He rode back down the slope, choosing a canyon that veered off at an angle toward the north and east. It should bring him out somewhere on the eastern edge of the Conejo or, possibly, just beyond the pass above Calabasas.

He rode disconsolately. About midmorning he came into a cuplike depression in the mountains circled by a jagged wall of jumbled rocks. They combed the sky above like fangs, boulders the size of houses lined against the sky or projecting precariously from the canyon walls. The sun beat down in the cup, reflecting up from the yellow rocks, a torture to the eyes.

Blaise had ridden perhaps halfway across the rocky floor when a rifle cracked sharply, the bullet kicking up gravel just ahead, the echoes bounding back and forth among the rocks. Blaise jerked the reins and his hand slashed down to his Colt, his eyes lifting to the fanged ramparts far above. Sun blinded him and a mocking voice poured laughter down the walls.

170

A rifle spoke from another direction and the slug buzzed spitefully by, smashing against a distant rock and whining off. Blaise sat with his Colt lifted and laughter again mocked him.

"There can be more, *señor*," a voice called.

"Who are you?" Blaise demanded.

"Tiburicio Vasquez. We met once before, *señor*. *Dios*, had I known it was you, I would have promised your ears to the man who hired me."

"Show yourself!" Blaise challenged, and Vasquez laughed.

"In my good time, and my place, *amigo*. You have been watched since last night. We did not think you would find us."

"Where's Hal King? If you've killed him, I'll climb those rocks after you!"

"You'd die within a foot of where you stand," Vasquez answered. "Your friend is safe in Calabasas with a message for you."

"You've turned Hal loose!"

"Free as air, *señor*. Free as you are . . . at the moment."

"Is he hurt?"

"A flesh wound that is healing, no more."

Blaise slowly lowered the Colt and shoved it in the holster. He had glimpsed but one slight puff of smoke but didn't doubt that a dozen more rifles covered him. He was at Vasquez's mercy, and he knew it. But his voice remained steady and clear.

"What message did you send with Hal?"

"Very short, *señor*. Leave your rancho. Get out of this country. Go where you will, but ride far and never come back."

"You kidnapped Hal for that . . ."

"Next time there will not be a kidnap. There will be bullets, maybe in the night, or maybe in the day from a distant rock. *Quien sabe?*"

Blaise felt baffled. "Why do you want me out of the country?"

"I, *señor! Por el diablo*, I don't care if you stay or go, except for that little matter of the stage. That I would like to settle someday. But I have a patron, *señor*. He has paid me very well. *Bueno*, then I give value for his gold. You do not leave, I see that you stay in these mountains, where a bullet catch you. *Vaya con dios!*"

Blaise waited. There was silence. He carefully scanned the ramparts, could see no movement. He called, there was no answer. Vasquez was gone, his men with him. Blaise waited a few moments longer and then lifted the reins and touched the horse gently with his spurs. He rode out of the cup unmolested.

He tried to find some way of climbing to the ridge. Twice he cut into draws that promised to lead upward but both of them ended in cul-de-sacs and he had to return to the main trail.

It was close to sundown by the time he had cleared the mountains, rode through Calabasas and threaded the last canyon to the rancho. Lights blazed a friendly welcome and Blaise wearily dismounted, turned his horse into the corral. The door opened and Allen's big bulk showed against the light.

172

"Blaise? . . . Hal's here."

Blaise felt weariness flow out of him. He hurried to the bunkhouse. Allen moved aside and Blaise entered. He stood across the room, his arm bandaged. He grinned sheepishly at Blaise.

"I'm a hell of a partner," he said.

Blaise strode across the room. "You're all right?"

Hal indicated his arm. "Bullet-nicked, that's all."

Blaise stepped back, relief showing on his face. "Vasquez trapped me in the mountains. He said he'd let you go, but I didn't completely believe him."

Hal's face darkened. "He let me go, about a mile from here. I'm to tell you to get the hell out of these parts and stay out, me with you. If we don't, then we can figure on a bushwhack any time, any place."

"Where's his hideout?" Blaise asked. Hal cursed a little.

"They rode me over the pass from Calabasas and into the mountains, helpless as a roped dogie. Then they blindfolded me. Next I could see, I was locked in a shack."

"No window?"

"One, with a cliff wall maybe fifty feet away. I couldn't tell nothing, Blaise. They blindfolded me when they took me out. That's all I know."

"Damn' little," Blaise murmured.

"If I had an idea where it was, I'd sure ride in and clean me up some *bandidos*. I want a crack at those gents."

Blaise looked up, half smiling. "Then we won't leave the country?"

"For a bunch like that!" Hal swore again, caught himself and sobered. "Vasquez is the gent who tried to rob the stage. He holds that against us . . . said if he hadn't been hired, he'd start gunning us right away."

"Who hired him?"

"He never said. I tried to pump him but it didn't do no good. Could be Leonis."

"Did the boys tell you about Slim?"

"A good man, Blaise. Tolliver says Leonis didn't kill him."

"He says so . . . and I half believe him. He says he had nothing to do with Vasquez, either."

Hal tugged at his ear lobe. "Maybe he didn't. I figure Leonis would use his own crew for any dirty work. But who, Blaise, if it wasn't him?"

"I'd give an arm for an answer to that one," Blaise growled.

"Someone's coming," Uhl said suddenly and started to the door. Blaise heard the swift beat of hoofs and he grabbed the boy's arm, checking him. He bent down and blew out the lamp.

"Cover the windows," he snapped. "It could be trouble."

He moved to the door, palming the gun from his holster. He edged it open. Four or five riders came down the slope from the ridge above, making no attempt to conceal themselves. Blaise stood within the black shadow of the building, watching the silver-lit horsemen.

"Randell!" a man called. "Blaise Randell!"

Blaise shouted an answer, not moving from the shadows. The men came on, drew rein and then hastily dismounted. Hal spoke from the darkness just within the room.

"Las Montanas! That big gent's Raikes."

"Thatcher?" Blaise called.

"It's me, Randell. Rennie here?"

"Rennie!" Blaise holstered his gun and strode out into the moonlight. "Was she supposed to be?"

Thatcher came toward him, then halted, looking around as though he expected to find his daughter. "I . . . thought she might be. She went riding this afternoon and has never returned. There was a chance she was over here."

Blaise turned to the house where Hal and the others stood near the door. Tolliver answered before he could ask the question.

"We never saw any sign of her."

Thatcher passed his hand over his face.

"Raikes trailed her, after we began to worry. Her tracks joined with those of maybe half a dozen riders and that was the end of it. We — thought maybe she'd met with some of you boys and had come here. She's lost. What'll we do?"

"Where'd you lose the trail, Raikes?" Blaise asked.

"About five-six miles back, south of Calabasas."

Blaise felt panic rise. To be lost in these mountains was bad enough, but Blaise thought of Vasquez ranging the hills and of what might have happened. He turned on his heel and strode back to the shack, Thatcher following him.

He lit the lamp as the men crowded in. Thatcher's eyes looked hollowed.

"We'll eat and ride," Blaise said grimly. "Make sure your cartridge loops are filled."

CHAPTER
FIFTEEN

In the bright moonlight, Raikes had no trouble leading them to the place where Rennie's trail had blended with that of other horsemen. Thatcher explained that his men had hunted the near-by canyons and slopes, calling her name, firing their guns.

"She'd have answered . . . unless she was hurt."

Nevertheless, the men spread out, beating the brush again, and gunshots echoed now and then in the hope that she would reply. At midnight the men returned to the rendezvous, weary and tired, Blaise and Thatcher both openly worried.

"Could someone have kidnapped her?" Thatcher demanded.

Blaise hesitated. "It could happen." He told about Hal's capture and return. "Vasquez's men were in the neighborhood."

Thatcher's jaw tightened. "If they've harmed her —"

Blaise checked him. "I don't think they will. We'll wait until daylight and see if we can follow the trail."

"If we can't?" Thatcher asked. Blaise shrugged.

"Then we return to Las Montanas and wait. It's all we can do. But I'd bet my last dollar Vasquez will ask for ransom."

The men rolled up in blankets. Blaise and Thatcher slept very little. Blaise finally sat up and rolled a cigarette. He lit it and stared out into the moonlight, hugging his knees.

He faced the fact that Rennie had become of supreme importance to him. It had happened quietly, almost without his knowing it, but the panic he had felt when Thatcher had come with news of her disappearance had fully revealed it to him. Blaise studied the glowing end of his cigarette, seeing the deep violet eyes again, the trim figure, hearing the overtones of her voice.

His thought moved slowly to the girl's background. There was Las Montanas, a ranch huge enough to take a man's breath, but quite evidently of minor importance to the Thatchers. Compared to Las Montanas, Blaise's own ranch was of postage-stamp size, and now more than half burned. That represented all Blaise had in the world. Thatcher could buy him a dozen times over and hardly realize the money was gone. A giant and a pygmy, Blaise thought wryly, and the pygmy had come to love the giant's daughter.

Melanie . . . he recalled how he had dreamed of her, planned a life with her; and now Rennie had wholly taken her place. Blaise wondered if his emotions and feelings were as sincere as he had always believed. He could not honestly condemn himself. Without volition he had fallen in love with Rennie. It was no more than a simple fact but tremendous in its implications. And, an equally hard and cold fact, he might as well set himself to see Rennie go out of his life, too. There'd be a wealthy man from the East someday, one of the class

178

she knew. When he came, Rennie would vanish. He made a wry face in the darkness, ground out the cigarette, and rolled up in his blanket again.

As soon as the morning light was sufficient, Blaise studied the trail. The horsemen had come from the direction of Blaise's rancho. Rennie's tracks came in from the north and east, blended with the others at a spot where the horses had milled around. Her trail never emerged again.

The men followed the trail as it led westward, deeper into the mountains. After a couple of hours, Blaise was certain that they followed Vasquez's men. The bandit would be careful not to lead trailers into his hideout, and Blaise recalled the ease with which he had been trapped in the rock canyon. There must be a hundred other places where such an ambush could be set. Blaise wanted to press on, but his better judgment intervened. He finally drew rein and the others pressed in close around him.

"It's Vasquez, all right. We'll lose the trail further on and there'll be no chance of finding him."

Thatcher, white stubble showing on his cheeks, looked worriedly up toward the ridges, seeing the hopelessness of the situation. He turned to Blaise.

"We ride back?" he asked despondently. Blaise dropped his hand on the older man's shoulder.

"To Las Montanas. Vasquez will know who she is and he'll smell money down wind. He won't harm anything of value to him."

Thatcher looked around once more. "I hope to God you're right, Blaise."

179

They turned back, threading the canyons the long way to Las Montanas. Blaise turned his horse into the corral with the rest and followed Thatcher up to the big main house. The old man ordered the Mexican woman to prepare breakfast with a great deal of strong coffee. He showed Blaise to a room and then disappeared. Half an hour later, Blaise descended to the dining room where a big breakfast had been placed on the table. Thatcher, cleaned and shaved, stood by the window. Both men sat down but they ate very little, though the coffee steadily diminished.

Thatcher drained the last cup and stared heavily out the window. He sighed, caught himself and turned to Blaise. "When do you think Vasquez will come?"

"He'll send a messenger as soon as he thinks the uproar has quieted down. It might be tonight, or tomorrow. But he'll come. We can only wait."

"I hope you're right." Thatcher moved restlessly. "Have you learned anything about the Chavez business?"

Blaise shook his head. "Nothing definite, except that Leonis claims he had nothing to do with it."

"You believe him?"

"I want to," Blaise admitted.

"Does he suggest anybody?"

"No one . . . and no proof. Just his flat word, and you can take it or be damned. That was always his way."

"There are men like that," Thatcher nodded. "I guess you could count me among 'em. If he's honest with himself, he could be telling the truth. Or he could be lying."

180

"Either way," Blaise admitted. He told about Slim Starling and Hal's kidnapping and all that had led therefrom.

"Ordered out," Thatcher said when Blaise finished. "Leave or be killed. Leonis did that once before, you tell me."

"But in person," Blaise said quickly, "and he sent his own riders after us. He didn't hire a man like Vasquez to do his kidnapping and bushwhacking."

"I wonder if Rennie's disappearance is part of the pattern."

"I don't think so," Blaise replied. "She ran into Vasquez, and he saw a chance to cash in."

Thatcher sighed. "Blaise, it's important to me that you clear yourself of the Chavez murder."

"Important?"

"I — can't say why, just yet." He arose and walked to the window. "Las Montanas can be a great rancho, perhaps like those of the old days of the Spanish range, when a man owned hundreds of thousands of acres. It could be another King ranch, stretching from the sea to the Valley, over into the Conejo."

"That's big," Blaise said, awed.

"I've made a fortune," Thatcher still looked out the window. "Now I want to relax. But if I do anything I want to be a success. Anything else would make me feel I'm getting too old to see and think clearly. Las Montanas will pay for itself and grow.

"It will be a domain for my heirs. They can grow up here, be one with the land and the country. Their roots will be here and they will not have to claw their way upward in a smoky, industrial city as I did. That will be good."

He turned. "All this will go to Rennie. She's my whole family." Suddenly his eyes grew moist. "Blaise, nothing can happen to her! It can't!"

"I understand," Blaise said quietly. "It won't happen. You'll see."

Thatcher caught himself up, but the conversation had ended. They set themselves to wait for news from Vasquez.

The day dragged by. Blaise went out to the corral and busied himself with minor tasks. He constantly watched the road, or the ridges for sign of a messenger.

The evening meal was silent and brooding, neither man eating much. Thatcher led the way to the library and each settled in a chair, deep in his own thoughts. Twice Blaise left the room, going down the long hall to the door and outside. The stars were bright but there was no moon. He could sense rather than see the ocean in the distance. Lights burned at the foot of the slope in the mens' quarters, but all was quiet. Each time Blaise returned, shaking his head at Thatcher's questioning look.

They had been sitting glumly for a long time when someone pounded on the front door, pushed it open, and came hurrying down the hall. Blaise and Thatcher were both on their feet when Raikes came striding into the room.

"We caught us a night rider," he said shortly, "out beyond the corrals. He wants to see the Boss."

"From . . . Rennie?"

"He won't say nothing except to you, but I think he is."

"Then for God's sake, bring him in!"

Raikes nodded, turned on his heel, called an order and soon boots sounded loud.

"This is him," Raikes said. Two Montanas riders shoved a third man forward. He caught himself, sneered and spat deliberately at their feet. Raikes's face turned scarlet and his big hand struck out, the fingers tightening on the man's neck.

"Leave him be!" Thatcher snapped.

Raikes stepped back and the man rubbed his dirty neck, some of his braggadocio returning. Blaise read in him a mixture of bad Indian and a dozen other border breeds, a *cholo*. His face was pockmarked, his eyes shifting. His shirt was filthy, his high-crowned hat ragged around the greasy brim. Black, wiry hair matted over his forehead. But his gun belt and holster were beautifully tooled, the loops filled with bright cartridges. Raikes had taken the man's weapon long since. He looked from Blaise to Thatcher with increasing boldness.

"'*Dias*," he said at last. "Who is *patron* of Rancho de Las Montanas?"

"I am," Thatcher replied. The man studied him, then glanced at the others.

"I have a word for you, *señor*, if these *perros* . . ." He shrugged and grinned at Raikes's thunderous scowl. Thatcher waved the men away but Raikes protested.

"He's a damn sidewinder if I ever saw one. We'd better stay around."

"Randell's here," Thatcher said and the men reluctantly left. Thatcher faced the *cholo* again, who looked admiringly around at the furnishings, cupidity showing in his appraising glance. "Your message?"

"Ah, *si*. I have come from Señor Tiburicio Vasquez. He has a guest."

"An unexpected one," Blaise said dryly. The *cholo* peered up at him.

"*Si*, that is right. She is very lovely and Tiburicio is most pleased. But she will stay maybe a short time, maybe a long time, *quien sabe?*"

"Get to the point," Thatcher snapped.

"Señor Vasquez think that perhaps she stay short time if he is repaid for . . . the comfortable *casa* he provide for her and the food. It is to be considered, *señor*. She is well, untouched. That is to be considered, *señor*."

"And the board and lodgings?" Thatcher demanded.

The *cholo* lifted his shoulders in a characteristic gesture. "For some less, for some more. For Señorita Thatcher we have given our best, *por Dios*. Señor Vasquez has set a very reasonable price . . . ten thousand dollars."

"Ten thous — ! Why, damn you . . ."

Thatcher lunged for him, but Blaise checked the older man. "Easy! Easy! Let me handle this."

Thatcher stared at him and then, amazingly, his nether lip quivered beneath the iron-gray mustache. He turned abruptly to the window. In a moment he straightened though he didn't look around.

"It's Rennie. Her safety. Of course —"

184

Blaise took a quick stride to his side and spoke low. "Wait a minute. Tell the man you'll decide by morning. Keep him here."

"Blaise, I can't. It's taking a chance."

"I don't think so. Do as I say. I'll explain later. If you don't agree then let him go with word to Vasquez. But stall until we can talk alone."

Thatcher looked around, eyes still misted. "Call Raikes. He'll be just outside the door."

Blaise strode to the outer door and brought Raikes and his two men back. Thatcher had already spoken to the *cholo*, who looked uncertain and suspicious. Thatcher signaled to take the man away.

"Hold him until morning. Then bring him here."

They led the bandit away and Thatcher walked to his chair, sat down heavily. He looked up at Blaise.

"Now what? What did we gain?"

"Time," Blaise said. "I'm saddling up and leaving right away. In the morning, tell that *cholo* you'll agree to the ransom, to anything. Then turn him loose."

"But you didn't want —"

"To pay the ransom," Blaise nodded, "nor risk Rennie. We won't do either." He described quickly and graphically his search for Hal. "I lost the trail, but Vasquez's hideout is close around. It's bound to be. This *cholo* will ride direct to Vasquez. I'll trail him to the hideout and then wait for you and the men."

"But how will we know where you are!"

"Just beyond the Calabasas path, I'll start blazing trail — one rock atop another with a third to the side to mark the direction. Raikes will be able to follow it."

"I don't like it. If we attack, Vasquez will kill Rennie."

"We won't attack the hideout. Tell this *cholo* Vasquez is to bring the girl out. You'll meet him somewhere along the trail with the money. But give the *cholo* a long start. Then come riding with the men. We'll be waiting when Vasquez comes out of the hideout. We'll have Rennie before he'll know what hit him."

Thatcher tugged at his lip and chewed the end of his mustache. Blaise waited, poised, impatient. Thatcher finally dropped his hand.

"You could make a bad mistake, boy."

Blaise nodded and his eyes grew soft, sobered. "I know how you feel about Rennie. I'll play it safe all the way along."

"All right. We'll follow the *cholo*. But if at any time it looks bad for Rennie, I'll pay ten thousand without a quiver. Understand that."

"Yes, sir. Tell Raikes to follow my sign, starting south of the road, just beyond the pass. I'll be riding now."

"Good luck." Thatcher arose and took his hand.

Blaise stopped briefly at the big bunkhouse down below, to tell Hal the general direction to take and landmarks that would guide him.

Then he rode on. Calabasas was dark and ghostly when he rode through; only a dog barked, muffled from within a shed. The store fronts watched him blankly and with secretive foreboding as he passed by and started the climb into the pass. Just beyond, he dismounted and made the first of the signs with the three stones.

He stopped again at the place where he had plunged into the hills and made another sign, indicating the canyon. He retraced his former trail in his search for Hal, marking each turn. A chill set upon the night as darkness increased its cold grip on the world just before dawn.

At last Blaise came to the place where he had lost the trail. Gray light streaked the eastern horizon and a wind lifted, funneling through the canyons, stirring the sage and the few trees.

Blaise knew he was close to Vasquez's hideout. He had lost the trail here once before in the maze of canyons but, as the crow flies, it had not been too far distant to the rocky depression where Vasquez had challenged him. Somewhere in this serpentine maze of canyons and peaks Vasquez held Rennie, and his messenger would be bound to come this way.

By the uncertain light, Blaise found a big clump of mesquite on a gentle slope. He could command the entrance to the meadow and the maze of canyons at the far end, the rocky, dry stream bed to the place where it turned sharply and plunged into the hills.

He set himself to wait. Light increased and the sky glowed with the coming of the sun. Warmth crept back into Blaise's chilled frame. From his hiding place he scanned the line of the ridges around him.

Time dragged and Blaise began to feel something of doubt. Perhaps he had followed a trail to this point, but that did not necessarily mean that there was but one entrance to Vasquez's lair. The messenger might take another course and pass on the far side of one of the high ridges. He pushed the thought aside. Vasquez had undoubtedly taken the direct trail from Calabasas to the hideout with Hal, and the messenger would do the same. That would bring him into sight just below.

But the gnawing uncertainty returned, to be pushed down again, only to return once more. Blaise had to fight down an impulse to leave the shelter of the mesquite and scout around.

The sun came up over the eastern peaks, flooding the meadow with hot, yellow light. The breeze had died and summer heat built up within the meadow until late in the afternoon.

Suddenly Blaise's horse lifted its head, ears pricked forward. Instantly Blaise jumped to his feet and clamped his hand over the animal's nose, his eyes intent down the slope.

A man came through the cleft and into the meadow. It was the pockmarked *cholo*, now rearmed. The man did not so much as glance up the slope and, instead of heading across the meadow to the canyons beyond, turned into the stony creek bed. He followed the watercourse around its sharp turn and disappeared.

Blaise's eyes widened in surprise. He whipped around and jumped into the saddle. He rode directly down the slope to the watercourse and turned into it. He stopped a moment to set another sign and then went on.

He rounded the turn. The watercourse had broken a narrow cleft through a wall of clay and soft sandstone, a knife-cut of a ravine where Blaise could have touched either wall. Here the stones had disappeared to be replaced by a solid footing of sheet rock, still leaving no sign of a trail.

Blaise rode cautiously because of the man ahead, hidden from sight by the twisting turns of the ravine. It widened, turned sharply again and opened into a wide meadow.

Blaise pulled up, still just within the mouth of the ravine. He saw his man across the meadow, heading directly toward another solid wall of rock. As Blaise watched, he heard a distant shout, and movement on the far rock rampart caught his eye. A man stood lined against the sky. The messenger lifted his arm in a swift salute and rode on, disappearing into a narrow crevice.

Blaise sat quite still, triumph lighting his eyes. Across the meadow was the long-sought entrance. Somewhere behind him, Hal and the Las Montanas men followed. Gradually the triumph faded as Blaise studied the meadow and the high rock barrier beyond. The guard above would instantly spot any approaching riders.

Blaise looked slowly along the line of the ridge, then studied the intervening space. A man on horse would be instantly seen, but a man afoot would find brush and rock to conceal him. He could cross the meadow at a long angle and reach a broken talus slope perhaps half a mile north of the guard's position.

If the guard could be removed without alarm then Las Montanas would find an open doorway to the hideout. Blaise dismounted and picketed the horse several yards in from the mouth of the ravine. He looked thoughtfully across the meadow, then hitched at his gun belt and started forward.

CHAPTER
SIXTEEN

It took a long time to work across the meadow; moving swiftly to a bush, waiting, and watching the far ridge, then edging forward, using scant cover to a huge boulder, skirting it and darting to another bush. Blaise made the talus slope without giving alarm so far as he knew. There was the chance that, if the guard had binoculars, Blaise's progress had been followed step by step and that the guard waited among the rocks just above.

He crouched against the big boulders at the foot of the broken slope and searched the jumbled rocks for some sign of the guard. If the man had remained where Blaise had first seen him, then Blaise was well out of his line of vision. Blaise threw a swift glance at the sun, trying to determine how soon Hal and the boys would ride in the far side of the meadow. It could not be long.

He rubbed his hands along his levis, studying the lay of the rocks, the little rain-formed ledges and washes that would give him a path of sorts, the few bushes that would afford a grip.

He started up, watching the rim, half expecting the blast of a rifle. None came as he worked on up, beginning to breathe heavily on the steep slope, sweat staining his shirt between the shoulder blades and misting his face.

He halted just below the top, left hand clinging to a bush, the right sliding the Colt out of the holster. He removed his hat and peered over the ledge. It was flat and quite wide. Blaise looked toward the ravine that cut it, but could see only scattered sage and rock. He scrambled the few feet to the top and stood at a crouch, listening, looking down on the meadow he had just crossed.

He worked his way along the ridge, careful not to disturb the brush so that the guard would be warned. It was slow work and Blaise had to check his impatience.

Suddenly the brush thinned, stopped completely. There was no longer any cover. About ten yards away was a circular depression, wind and rain-worn into the soft sandstone. A man lay sprawled there, looking out toward the meadow, a rifle shoved forward, resting on the lip of the rim. Blaise measured the distance. He could never get across the open space and reach the guard before the man turned and fired. That single shot would undo everything.

He heard a sound to his right and shrank back into the bushes. A man came from the far rim. The guard turned and stood up as the second man appeared, who was also armed with Colt and rifle.

"It is time," the guard growled. "*Por Dios*, you're an hour late."

"Martinez came," the second shrugged. "Tiburicio says that we will soon have plenty pesos."

"I saw Martinez come through. So they will pay the ransom, eh!" He lost his ill temper at the thought, grinned, stretched and rolled a cigarette. "How is it to be done?"

"In the morning, we ride out. There will be a meeting. It is that simple." The second man glanced down into the valley. "There has been nothing?"

"Nothing but stray breezes that disturbed the bushes now and then. The chili is hot?"

"I just left it. On your way, Rafeal."

Rafeal nodded and moved away, dropping from sight over the far edge of the slope. The new man stood watching the meadow as the sun sank lower, scanning it carefully. Blaise waited, narrowly watching, impatient. But at last the man sank down into the depression, placed his rifle close to hand and rolled a cigarette before he rolled over on his stomach to guard the approaches comfortably.

Blaise still faced the problem of the open space and he knew that time grew shorter. He studied the distance and once more gave up the thought of a quick rush. He might slip up on the man but any slight noise would bring instant alarm. Blaise cast around him for some means of solving the problem.

He saw a big, jagged piece of sandstone a few feet away. He eyed it, then measured the distance. He picked up the rock, tested its weight and then slowly stood up. His eyes narrowed as he measured the distance, his muscles tensed.

The rock hurtled like a projectile straight for the high-peaked sombrero. At the same instant Blaise jerked his Colt from the holster and lunged forward. The guard's head turned and, a split second later, the rock caught him squarely against the side of the head. He dropped and then Blaise was on him, the gun barrel thudding with a solid sound against the man's skull. The guard didn't move.

Blaise crouched, listening, watching, and then hastily went to work. He took the man's Colt from the holster, dropped it and the rifle over the edge of the cliff. He ripped the man's shirt into long strips and quickly bound his hands and feet, made an effective gag that he tied securely around his head.

Blaise moved at a crouch across the ridge top. At the far edge he looked down into another meadow, this one as large as any he had seen in these mountains. To his left a narrow, knifelike canyon gave the only entrance. Blaise saw a line of shacks against the far wall and cook-fires made dots of orange light in the shadows of the far cliffs. A big corral held several horses.

Blaise drew back and considered the narrow pathway that led downward into the ravine. He studied the guard, tested his bonds and decided he would sleep indefinitely. He worked his way down to the bottom of the ravine, threaded it to the meadow he had just left and boldly walked across it to his horse. It would probably be hours before anyone came up to relieve the guard who had just been posted. In that time Thatcher and Las Montanas should be here.

The sun plunged behind the western peaks and a golden mantle spread over the sky, changing subtly to yellows, green and then a brilliant ruby interspersed with purple. Blue shadows crept into the meadow and the rocks of the canyon stood out boldly in this last, waning light of day.

Blaise heard hoof beats behind him and he swung around. He held his right hand near his gun as the sounds grew louder and the first horsemen turned the corner into his sight. Thatcher and Hal led the procession, Raikes and Allen just behind, the rest following. Thatcher instantly spurred forward.

"You've found her?"

"The hideout — and the guard's tied up. We just ride in."

"Thank God!" Thatcher breathed. "We had a little trouble following the sign."

Hal looked sharply at Blaise. "Any trouble with the guard?"

"An easy job," Blaise grinned. "We'd better get on. Someone just might take a notion to look around."

He led the way across the meadow and into the narrow portal of the hideout. There was no challenge. They came out into the meadow just at dusk, half light making objects uncertain. Lights glowed far ahead. Blaise reined in, spoke to Thatcher.

"We block the only way out. Rennie's somewhere up ahead in one of those cabins. I'd better take a look-see, so we'll waste no time getting to her."

"I'll go with you," Hal offered. Blaise shook his head.

"You take charge here. If anything happens, you'll know what to do. I won't be gone long."

He rode off into the gathering dusk, staying close to the cliff walls, in a long circle that would bring him on the camp from the south. A hundred yards from the nearest cabin, Blaise dismounted and ground-tied the horse. He palmed his gun into his hand and crept forward.

Men moved before the fires and he could hear loud talk. Someone strummed a guitar and he heard a burst of strident laughter. He reached the corner of the first cabin, edged to the lighted window and peered inside. Four men sat at a plank table playing poker.

Blaise faded back, moved around the rear corner and worked his way to the next cabin. It was dark and he tried vainly to peer in the window. He moved back, puzzled, wondering if he dared investigate the other shacks. The bandits talked and moved about but a few feet from him now.

Blaise slipped to the next shack to find the window boarded up. His fingers explored, made a slight scratching sound. Something stirred inside and he heard a frightened, sibilant —

"Who's that!"

Blaise froze but he felt relief flood him and he smiled widely in the darkness. He moved silently away from the cabin and back the way he had come. He reached his horse, pulled the reins over its head and stepped into the saddle. He reined around and moved slowly off until he was certain he was out of earshot. Then he set the spurs and raced away. He had found Rennie.

A sharp challenge pulled him up while still some yards from the entrance. Hal came cautiously forward until Blaise identified himself, then the others crowded in. Blaise quickly described the camp and Rennie's cabin.

"Thatcher, you and me will bear off to the left. Hal, you and the boys spread out. Move in slow, and give us a chance to reach Rennie. When you think we're set, say half an hour, hit 'em hard. If trouble breaks before then, ride in to cover us."

Thatcher followed Blaise out across the meadow. Again Blaise made a circle, this time a tighter one, and soon he reined in and ordered Thatcher to dismount. He pointed to the fires before the shacks.

"Be ready for trouble," he warned. "If the boys open up, work fast."

"You lead me to my daughter, son. I'll take care of the rest."

They moved toward the shacks, approaching them from the rear. Blaise cautioned Thatcher for silence as they hugged the cliff wall, edged by the first shack and the second. They drifted silently to the third and soon stood beside the boarded-up window. Again Blaise felt for the boards, hesitated, and rapped his knuckles sharply on the planks. Both men heard a stir inside and a muffled voice again asked, "Who's there?"

"Rennie!" Thatcher said in a hoarse, triumphant whisper.

"Dad!"

"You're all right?" Thatcher asked through one of the wide cracks. Her voice sounded stronger.

"Fine. But they'll kill you if they find you, Dad!"

"Blaise is here, and the boys."

"Blaise! With you?"

"Right beside me."

Blaise put his mouth close to the crack. "The boys'll hit the camp soon. Anyone in front of the shack?"

"The cook-fires, and they're all around them," she replied. "But no guard at the door."

"Good! I'm going to the side of the cabin. When the boys attack, stand back from the door. I'll shoot the lock off and get you out while Vasquez is busy."

"Be careful," she warned. "Blaise!"

"Yes?"

"I hoped maybe you'd come. Do be careful."

"I will."

He straightened, a warm glow in his heart. He motioned Thatcher to follow him and went to the corner, peering around it. A fire burned close, lighting up the space between the shacks. A couple of men walked by and Blaise jerked back into the shadows. A sharp voice challenged in a totally unexpected direction, off to his right from the shadows of the adjoining cabin.

"You! What you do there? Who are you? Come out in the light!"

Blaise and Thatcher stood immobile. Blaise caught a movement in the shadows. He lunged into Thatcher, throwing the old man to the ground as his hand streaked the Colt from the holster. A gun spat flame from the far shadows and the bullet thudded into the cabin wall. Blaise threw two fast slugs. Alarmed shouts sounded out in front.

Then hoofs thundered in the night, came rolling toward the cabins as a fierce, hoarse yell lifted. Guns

197

slammed from the outer darkness, raking the fires, the cabin, the confused bandits. Hell broke with a roar.

Blaise slammed another shot into the shadows, then dashed around the corner of the shack, racing for the front. Firelight showed a pandemonium of running men, lances of gun flame. Blaise jumped for the door, aimed the Colt at the heavy lock and slammed a bullet into it. It jumped and fell broken. Blaise jerked it loose and his shoulder crashed open the door.

Rennie came. He took her hand and, shielding her from the gunfire, moved to the corner of the cabin. A bullet came close, a second. Blaise saw a man standing not far away and recognized Vasquez. He lifted his Colt but the bandit leader whirled and dashed off into the darkness.

Blaise raced down the corridor between the cabins, Rennie beside him. Thatcher met them and the three plunged into the protecting darkness beyond the last faint glow from the fires. Blaise hurried them along to their horses. He ordered Thatcher to mount, take his daughter and head in a wide circle toward the entrance.

"But don't go close to the canyon mouth. Vasquez and his boys will be fighting to reach it, too. When it's over, I'll meet you."

He lifted Rennie to a seat behind her father. She looked down at him, her face a soft blur in the darkness. Her hand still held his.

"Blaise, come closer," she said. She bent down and kissed him, her hand against his cheek. "That's all the thanks I can give now."

198

Thatcher reined the horse around and raced away. Blaise stood transfixed, forgetful of the place and time. He gently touched his lips with his fingers. A sudden increase in the firing jerked him around. The bandits had formed a small fighting group near the cabins, Vasquez evidently having whipped them into some kind of order.

Blaise turned and jumped into the saddle. He hastily reloaded his gun and then set the spurs, racing down the slope, taking the bandits from the rear. He knocked over one man, sent a second reeling. He yelled, fired again.

The bandits, evidently precariously held only by Vasquez's commands, sent a few scattering shots Blaise's way, then broke and ran. At that moment Hal and the others raced into the firelight, streaked along the row of cabins in hot pursuit. Blaise veered to join them, hoping to cut off all escape at the narrow entryway.

There was sporadic firing, a drumming chase through the darkness, but it was soon over. Raikes and his men pursued the bandits through the ravine, but once beyond the far meadow, there were a thousand scattered hiding places in the hills.

Blaise, Hal and the five men from Simi drew rein at the canyon mouth. Silence fell on the meadow, almost strange and fearsome after the thunder that had just filled it. Blaise called into the darkness and Thatcher answered. He came riding up, Rennie still clinging tightly to him.

"Any of them left?" Thatcher asked.

"We'll see," Blaise answered. "There's a man up on the cliffs. Allen, you and Denver can bring him down. We'll see what's left around the cabins."

They rode to the cabins, alert, not sure what they would find. A man called from one of the shacks and, by the dying fires, they saw him sitting on a step, holding tightly to one arm. Another lay sprawled not far away.

Blaise spurred ahead, Hal and the others following, leaving Thatcher and his daughter behind. The wounded man was a Montanas rider and so was the dead man.

"But we paid for him," the wounded man said between set teeth. "There's two dead'ns over there beyond the fires and a couple are moaning like deserted dogies down the line."

Tolliver worked on the wounded man while the others searched the camp. They found three dead bandits, one far beyond the fire, and two wounded. There was no sign of Vasquez. Raikes came riding in with his crew, all of them tired and dejected.

"They scattered from hell to breakfast," Raikes reported. "No chance of catching 'em. The hangman'll get 'em someday, though."

They rounded up some stray horses in the meadow, lashed the dead men and tied the prisoners securely to their saddles. Thatcher came up to Blaise just as they were ready to ride out. He made a sweeping gesture toward the cabins.

"Do we leave the camp for Vasquez to come back to?"

Blaise grinned and shook his head. He picked up a burning brand from the fire and pitched it inside the door of the first cabin. Instantly flames leaped and spread. Blaise used another brand on the next cabin and soon the whole line was ablaze. The riders drew off and watched the flames lick high.

"No wind," Blaise told Thatcher, "and a bare cliff wall behind. It'll do no more damage than destroy a rat's nest."

They watched until the shacks collapsed in a shower of sparks and then Blaise neck-reined his horse and rode toward the entrance. They stopped on the way out to pick up the trussed guard and then rode on. Thatcher and Rennie came up beside Blaise.

"A good night's work," Thatcher said.

"But not finished," Blaise answered. "We'll hear more from Vasquez."

CHAPTER
SEVENTEEN

The return from the mountains was long and tedious. Horses and riders were tired and yet the endless miles of twisting canyons stretched out ahead. There was some talking at first, but soon all of them lapsed into silence. Some dozed as they rode along, others slumped wearily, the reaction setting in from the hurried ride and the swift, tense battle.

But at last they came out of the hills, climbed the pass and dropped down into Calabasas. It was well after midnight and the town was dark. But so many horsemen passing down the street caused lights to spring up in the houses. Windows raised and alarmed voices questioned the riders. A single light burned before the livery stable and Blaise turned toward it. The hostler came out and pulled up short, staring at the cavalcade in alarm. Blaise wearily dismounted.

"We raided Vasquez's hideout," he started, "and we've —"

"You what!" the hostler gasped. "Vasquez!"

"Him," Blaise said dryly. "We've got three live bandits that need a trial. Is there a safe place to keep 'em?"

The hostler stared. Townsmen came up, curious and excited. They asked questions that the riders answered in brief monosyllables. The storekeeper pushed forward.

"The warehouse behind my store is solid enough to hold 'em."

"Lead the way," Blaise turned and followed the man to a stout building behind the store. The three bandits were herded inside. The storekeeper produced a heavy padlock that he closed through the hasp. Blaise took the key, weighed it, looked up at Thatcher.

"Can some of your boys stand guard?"

Thatcher instantly named four and Blaise passed the key to one of them. He turned to the storekeeper. "Tell Leonis I'll see him tomorrow, before sundown."

"I won't see Leonis."

"Then send a messenger. I'll see him either here or at Scorpion. It doesn't matter."

Blaise remounted and the cavalcade rode out, leaving an excited town behind them. They came to Blaise's rancho and he offered what small accommodations he had to Thatcher and his crew. The old man refused, wanting to get on home, to make doubly sure that Rennie would be safe. Rennie, now on a horse of her own, edged in closer.

"I'll look for you at Las Montanas," she said.

"I'll come."

"Be sure." She wheeled the horse away and spoke over her shoulder. "I'll be waiting."

Las Montanas rode off into the darkness and Blaise stood listening to the fading sound of the hoofs. Then he glanced up at the stars, determining the time, and walked wearily into the bunkhouse. The men were too tired for speech and soon all of them were in their bunks.

Blaise stretched out, feeling fatigue creep into his muscles and joints. He was so tired that it was difficult to find sleep. He thought of Rennie, safe now on her way home, and he recalled the unspoken things in her voice when she said she'd be waiting for his visit. It gave him a glowing, warm feeling until once more he faced the cold fact of the immense differences between them. She'd go East someday and Blaise would see no more of her. It saddened him and then, suddenly, he was sound asleep.

It was late when Blaise awakened. Allen and Tolliver were already up and fully dressed. Hal whistled loudly from the washbench just outside the door; Denver and Uhl struggled up from their blankets a moment after Blaise awoke. They had breakfast and then Blaise passed around the makings.

"I want to thank all of you for taking a hand against Vasquez. It was none of your battle, but we sure needed your help."

"Thanks, nothing!" Uhl exclaimed and smiled impishly. "You think we could leave a pretty lady in bad trouble?"

Allen chuckled, his fat jaws quivering. "The young'n's said it for us, I reckon. Forget it, Blaise."

Blaise nodded, but they knew he wouldn't forget. He hitched forward, leaning his arms on the table. "There's no use wasting your time around here. You wanted

Valley land, and Leonis says you can have it so far as he's concerned."

"You think he meant it?" Denver asked. Blaise shrugged.

"It's for us to find out. If you file claims, it'll call his bluff. If Leonis starts trouble, it'll be then."

Tolliver reflectively stroked his stubbly chin, then nodded. "No use waiting. It's what we come for — that and Slim's killer."

"We'll get him, too, sooner or later," Blaise promised.

"What'll you be doing?" Allen asked.

"Paying Scorpion a visit."

"Then we don't ride off no place," Denver said flatly, "except to Scorpion with you."

"No," Blaise shook his head. "It'll be just me and Hal. You boys'd only get his dander up." Blaise rose. "You ride to the Valley and pick your claims. Take your time, for you're sure welcome to stay here. When you know what you want, ride to Los Angeles."

He walked away to prevent further argument. He and Hal were saddled up first and they rode leisurely out of the canyon and down to the Valley floor, taking the road to Calabasas.

They stopped at the store, checking the prisoners and the guards. The bandits were still securely locked up, and one of the Montanas riders told Blaise there had been constant excitement in the town.

"They keep coming and staring at the building, like they could see through the walls. There's been talk of a necktie party, right out there at that old oak before the store, but it's just talk."

"Anything from Scorpion?"

"Nothing definite. I heard someone sent word, but I ain't seen any riders come in."

Blaise nodded, satisfied. "We'll get out there before Scorpion can stir up trouble. Keep those renegades safe for a court and a hangnoose. Thatcher'll send some boys down to take 'em to Los Angeles."

Blaise signaled to Hal and they mounted and rode north out of town. Scorpion ranch lay in the low rolling hills, a pleasant country of wide natural pastures, of low grassy knobs and small canyons that ended almost before they started in irregular fields of grass nestled between the hills. Scorpion actually hemmed the town in to the north, but there was no sign of rider or cattle until Blaise and Hal had ridden for a couple of miles.

They came out of a small draw and saw cattle grazing, sleek stock that made Hal's eyes gleam. Almost simultaneously four riders appeared on the trail ahead. They saw Blaise, paused, and then came on at a fast trot. Even at a distance, Blaise could sense their suspicion. They drew rein a few yards off, four hard-faced men with narrowed eyes.

"Strayed, ain't you?" their spokesman said.

"This is Scorpion," Blaise answered. "I rode this way."

"Then ride back, mister. We don't like strangers."

"I'll see Leonis first."

"Sure?"

"If I have to fight through the whole crew," Blaise nodded. The man straightened, angered. He glanced at

206

Hal, studied Blaise and then looked sidelong at his companions.

"I reckon we'll ride along."

"Suit yourself," Blaise said evenly and urged his horse forward. The riders parted, letting him and Hal through. They fell in behind, riding silently and without talk. Blaise paid no apparent attention to them, but Hal didn't like four suspicious men at his back.

The trail led deeper into the hills and finally ended in the big ranch yard itself. The house was of adobe, a squat, low building, made spacious by the indiscriminate additions of wings. The thick walls looked ancient, the tiles dulled by many, many suns. The Spanish had built this type of rancho in the long distant past, and Leonis had inherited it from his wife's people. As they rode up, the big man came out from the shadow of the arched entryway.

He shielded his eyes from the sun with his hand, suddenly dropped it and came striding down the slight slope to the fence. Two or three men appeared from around the house and more followed slowly. Hal half lifted his hand toward his holster, then dropped it.

"It's the gent you rode out of Calabasas," one of the men said as Leonis came up. "He said he was going to see you or do some shooting."

"What in hell you do here!" Leonis demanded. "You have always been trouble. Get out."

Blaise leaned forward eyes level. "We need to lay cards face up, Leonis. You had me put away in jail, you grabbed land where you could, drove off your neighbors. Now you claim to be all sweetness and light."

"So?"

"You talk . . . but you ride me out of Calabasas. You use my rancho as a line camp and when I take over, it's burned. A man's killed in Simi. My partner is kidnapped — and now a woman. I'm warned to get out of the country or be bushwhacked. Kidnapping, land grabbing, arson, bushwhack and plain murder. I think you're behind it."

Leonis blinked. "You're crazy."

"Words ain't enough, Leonis. You talk fine but prove nothing."

"You don't have to take it, Boss," one of the riders said sharply. Leonis waved him to silence, studying Blaise. His thick lips pressed.

"Come into the house. Back to your work. I take care of this."

The main room was low and dark and dust lingered in the corners. There was a dilapidated grandeur about it, something still of the aloof pride of the days of Spain and Mexico. The massive chairs had been handmade, cow-skins stretched across seat and back. The table still held the remains of breakfast and an open tally book. Leonis sat down, motioned Blaise and Hal to take chairs. He tightly folded his big hands, looked grimly at Blaise.

"I have never take words like that before anyone, let alone my crew. I do not take it now, except I see that you believe these things. I tell you the truth, then you do what you want. But I do not wait next time to

208

explain if you still call me liar. What is this about a woman? What are these prisoners you bring to Calabasas and send word that I am to leave them alone? Why should I bother?"

"They're Vasquez's men. He's interfered twice now . . . to your advantage."

Leonis made an impatient gesture. "Give me facts, not what you think about them. I know nothing."

Blaise hesitated, decided to give the man the benefit of the doubt. He told about Rennie's kidnapping, and the attack on the hideout.

"And you blame me?" Leonis asked.

"I think Vasquez is your man. Maybe he took Rennie on the spur of the moment, but a split of ten thousand would help you."

Leonis placed his hands flat on the table. His eyes flashed but his voice remained calm. "I have done many things, perhaps. But I have never kidnapped a woman, or ordered it done, or shared any profit from it. You may believe it."

Blaise studied him closely. The calm tone, the indignant flash of the man's eyes almost convinced him, though some lingering doubt remained. "Vasquez does your work for you."

Leonis pulled himself from the chair in such haste that it fell to the floor. His big fist smashed on the table. "That is never so! I have tried to build a ranch here . . . once I thought to make it big to the mountains east and south and north. But I never use Vasquez. I will give you Scorpion riders to hunt him down and kill him."

"And these prisoners?"

"I would not raise a finger to help them." Leonis paused, looked at Blaise a long moment and then sat down. "But there are these other things that you believe of me. You drive my men from your rancho. You come back to live there, it is right they leave."

"They didn't talk that way."

"They did not know. I tell them they are not to go back, ever. It is your rancho . . . you have it. I drive you from Calabasas because I think you start gunning from the moment you return. I put you in jail. You want to get even. I want only to keep peace in Calabasas and this land."

"Once you didn't."

"Once I did not," Leonis agreed. "But then I have not nearly lost everything with flood and drought. I have not then understand this will not be big cattle country, that I have enough land for my own needs.

"I have not added land in years. I see it does me no good unless I hold empty land to sell maybe sometime. I do not have the money or patience for that. So, I do not set fire to your place. I do not have anyone killed in Simi, nor do I join with a dirty bandit to kidnap. That I don't do."

"You're asking me to believe a lot only on your own word," Blaise said finally.

"Is that not enough?" Leonis demanded.

"Hardly, under the circumstances."

Leonis jumped to his feet, eyes flashing. Then he caught control of himself. "Once more I am called a liar."

"No . . . I only want proof."

"I cannot give it. But maybe I tell you something that help you. Who is buying up homestead claims a little at a time over the past ten years? Who has bought tax-delinquent lands? I do not care who, but I do learn the old, vacant land out in the Valley is bought up, a bit here, a bit there."

Blaise watched him closely. Leonis leaned over the table, big hands supporting the trunks of his arms.

"Up toward Chatsworth, between there and the Mission, are the most farms. New . . . almost all in ten years. Who they buy from?"

"All right, who?" Hal interposed. Leonis paid no attention to him.

"I take advantage of what I find. Like I learn about Chavez when I think I want Valley land and I come to your rancho while you are gone."

"Then it *was* you!" Blaise exclaimed.

"I hunt, that only. We do not plant Chavez's gun because we never had it. Neither me nor any Scorpion man kill that bad hombre. But I find the weapon, I use it. You blame me for killing Chavez. I never did it. No man of mine did it. The trail you follow was never mine."

Leonis straightened with a sigh, looked from Hal to Blaise. "I have told you what I know. I want no more trouble, but I will help you hang Vasquez, for that brings peace at last to the Valley and to me. But do not ever again call me liar, or say that I do this or that. My patience is gone." He walked to the door. "More questions?"

211

Blaise thoughtfully shook his head. "None . . . right now."

"Then I think you go, perhaps. I will send Scorpion riders to help guard the prisoners and take them to Los Angeles for trial. It is a pleasure. I regret that Vasquez is not among them."

Blaise shoved his hat on his head, studied Leonis again, a long and searching stare. He spoke quietly to Hal.

"Wrong trail."

CHAPTER
EIGHTEEN

Blaise was hardly conscious of the slow ride back to Calabasas. He considered all that Leonis had told him, his protestations, his suggestions that Blaise investigate land ownership to find a reason for present troubles as well as a murder ten years old. Mark Davis had bought one section of Blaise's ranch at tax sale, but it didn't seem likely that Davis would profit from a burned ranch, a murder and a kidnapping.

They came to the town, rode to the livery stable and put up their horses. They checked the prisoners, to find that four more Montanas riders had come down to act as relief guards. It was high noon and Blaise felt hungry. He and Hal walked to a little café and had dinner. Finished, Blaise leaned back while Hal watched him and rolled a cigarette. Blaise tugged at his ear lobe.

"Leonis marked the end of a wrong trail," Hal said. "You believe him."

Blaise nodded. "I have to. He wasn't lying."

"No, but where does it put you?"

"In the dark," Blaise said wryly. "Look at what has happened. First, the fire. Then you're kidnapped and sent back with a warning there'll be bullets if we don't pull out of the country. Vasquez admits he's working for someone. Slim goes back to Simi to get a bunch together to homestead in the Valley again. He's shot. Rennie's kidnapped and held for ransom."

"I've tried to figure some sense to it," Hal said. "I always end up looking squarely at Leonis."

"So have I. But . . . you heard him. I believe him. So there has to be someone who gains every time something happens to us."

"This Rennie kidnapping," Hal said, "ain't part of the pattern. Vasquez just picked up something that came his way, that's all."

"I can see that," Blaise admitted, "but who gains with all the rest? Who wants us out of the country?"

Hal studied the end of his cigarette and gave Blaise a quick, sidelong glance. "If it ain't Leonis," he said quietly, "then I'd look somewhere else, right away. Maybe if you sort of worked a circle around this deal, it might come clear. Main thing is, someone profits if we're gone. Someone feels mighty uncertain and unhappy while we're around."

"Sure," Blaise said heavily, "but who?"

"It has to be someone close," Hal said.

Blaise nodded, and then a sudden light came in his eyes. He stared at Hal. Mark Davis? The idea had holes in it. Blaise shifted around in the chair, trying to reject the thought and yet unable to, still trying to fit Leonis into the picture but recalling the old man's denials. Blaise stared out into the sun-blasted street.

"You hold things down here, Hal," he said at last. "I'll be gone until tomorrow sometime."

"Where you heading?"

"Conejo. Maybe I didn't ask all the questions I should."

"Maybe I'd better ride along. You flush this gent we're hunting and you might need a lot of help."

"No, Hal. I'll go alone."

Hal rolled another cigarette, and spoke soberly. "I don't know much about the folks down here . . . not like you. But if it ain't Leonis, it'd be just one other." He took a long time with his match. "What about her?"

Blaise looked up. "I don't know, Hal."

"I'd rather it wouldn't be her," Hal said, testing each word. "She's married, and you —"

"Not now, even if she wasn't married," Blaise cut in.

"Well, that's a little something," Hal admitted. "I ain't said a word since I didn't know how things stood. But she caught me hard from the first time I seen her, Blaise. So I hope it ain't Mark Davis."

"Who else?"

"Leonis . . . lying fast and hard," Hal admitted. He made a wry face. "Ride on to Conejo. Tell me what you find out."

As Blaise came to the edge of town, he met five Scorpion men riding in. They nodded curtly, withdrawn, suspicious still though Leonis had said that Scorpion was not at war. Blaise half turned in the saddle, then thought that there were eight Montanas men and Hal if Scorpion planned treachery. He settled to the ride ahead.

He saw no sign of Mark when he rode by the house, so he continued up the road. Mrs. Case made him welcome and, soon after, Walt and Paul returned from the fields. Supper was ready and they ate immediately in that concentrated silence typical of ranch and farm. At last Paul sighed contentedly and sat back.

"What's the news?" he asked. Blaise sketched Rennie's kidnapping. They listened in stunned amazement and Walt spoke accusingly. "You said you'd call me. I never heard nothing . . . and all this was going on."

"Things moved too fast," Blaise answered with a smile. He glanced at Paul. "But when your work's done, I could use him a few days."

"Spring planting," Paul said and Blaise nodded, pleased that work would hold the boy for at least several weeks. The talk drifted on. At last the men moved into the front room, Walt helping his mother do the final chores.

"Paul, who got that land you were homesteading over in the Valley?" Blaise asked.

"Went open to claim again, I reckon, after I didn't prove up. It happened to all of us."

"Mark, too?"

"Sure, him with the rest so far as I know. But we proved up over here and done fine."

"What about Mark . . . and Melanie?" Blaise asked suddenly. Paul shifted uncomfortably and a stubborn line came to his jaw, then melted away.

"They're doing pretty good, I reckon. Mark's always broke, he says, though he's got one of the best farms around here. But he's always riding off, leaving Mel alone. She —"

He stopped and glanced toward the door, hearing the distant clink of dishes. "I ain't supposed to let on to no one, least of all you. But she ain't happy, Blaise, despite all Mark's done. She spends most of her time over here, and she don't talk much about Mark. That ain't natural in a woman. She's hiding something."

"What?" Blaise asked sharply. Paul sighed and shrugged.

"Maybe that Mark don't treat her good, or maybe that she knows she made a mistake. I reckon Maw and me are as much to blame as she, if the marriage ain't right. But it wasn't right a girl so young should wait for a man who'd never come back. You admit that, Blaise."

"I admit it," Blaise nodded. "But about Mark?"

"There's nothing I can say that I really know for certain. He's always gone, seems like . . . riding off, selling crops, making dickers. Mel's alone a lot. He's gone now."

"Where?"

"Said something about Simi. Left yesterday and ain't come back yet."

Maw Case came in and there was no more mention of Melanie and her problems. Blaise wanted to ride to the Davis house but he knew it was impossible this evening. For the sake of appearances, Maw and Paul would go along, and he'd get no chance to talk to Mel alone. He had to wait patiently until morning.

It was close to eight the next morning when he rode into the Davis yard, dismounted and knocked on the kitchen door. It opened and Melanie stared at him in surprise, pleasure lighting her eyes and her smile widening.

"Blaise! Come in." She threw the door wide. "I've had breakfast but there's always food for more."

"Your Maw fed me well. But coffee would be good."

"You didn't come over?" she asked, frowning, the light cotton dress revealing her full figure as she moved from table to stove.

"I wanted to," Blaise said. "But they'd come along."

She misread his meaning, stopping short at the stove and looking at him, her blue eyes soft, yet troubled. She came to the table and sat down across from him.

"I thought after you learned I'd married Mark, you'd hate me."

"No, I don't hate you, Mel. But I —"

"I've hated myself, Blaise! From the moment you returned I knew I'd made a horrible mistake. I think I knew it long before you came back, but I tried to make the best of a bad bargain."

"But Mark —"

"He doesn't love me, Blaise. He's always wanted the best land, the best horse, the best house in the district. He wanted the prettiest girl, and he got her. That's all that mattered. He loves himself, first and always. He isn't at all like you, Blaise."

"Mel, I — you're married to him. That makes a difference," Blaise tried to explain. She nodded slowly and her eyes misted.

"I know, Blaise. I should've waited for you. But the folks were against it. Mark acted like a perfect lover. I just gave in. I found out later just how important I was

218

to him. He loves himself first, then money, and he schemes and plans for it all the time. He's secretive, like a miser or a man afraid for the world to know him. Oh, Blaise, can't we do something!"

"I don't know what it would be, Mel. You see, I've found —"

"We could ride away, Blaise. We could be gone before anyone knew. We could go to Los Angeles, beyond Buenaventura. Anything, Blaise, anywhere!"

Blaise rubbed his hand over his eyes and arose from the table, pacing to the door and back. Melanie watched him, eyes wide and eager. She stood up, swinging around the chair, holding onto the back as she leaned forward toward Blaise. She was earnest and beautiful.

"I'll show you, Blaise, about Mark. Come here."

She turned and disappeared into the hall. Blaise reluctantly followed her. She called to him from beyond an open door. It was a bedroom, obviously a spare room, seldom used. The sunlight was dim and uncertain through a drawn blind. Mel opened the doors of a highboy and pulled a chair to it. She climbed up, groped far back on a shelf and pulled out a tin box. She opened the lid and held it down to Blaise.

"Look. There's what he loves . . . not me. Deeds, tax deeds."

Blaise took the box, strode to the bed and spread out the contents. Finally he looked up at Mel who had come to stand close beside him. His eyes shadowed as he gazed at her.

"How long, Mel?"

"He's been dealing in land for years, before we were married. He has traded and sold, bought more."

"You knew about this?"

"Only hints, Blaise. Mark would make hints about how he would be rich some day. But I found these just six months ago, accidentally when I decided to clean the room."

Blaise studied the deeds more carefully. He found Mark owned land around Chatsworth, in the Simi Valley, had tax deeds on parcels scattered over three valleys, and had even acquired the old Case homestead for a few dollars, the title dated but a short time after Leonis had driven his rivals from the San Fernando.

"I might have made a go of it," Melanie said. "He is handsome, and a wife can put a good front to a bad deal. But you came back, Blaise. Even then I've tried to carry out my bargain. But I can't, Blaise, knowing you're free, knowing you're just over the next range of hills."

"But, Mel —"

"I know now what you must have felt in prison, the way you wrote that you dreamed of me. I've . . . felt the same since you came back. I've been a prisoner, too, and I've dreamed."

Blaise swung to face her. "Mel, will you listen! You're married. I can't break up —"

"I can, Blaise," she said and he stared at her. She came close and put her arms around his neck. Her body was vibrant and warm.

"We were meant for each other, Blaise. I've learned that all over again."

220

He felt a deep sorrow for her. She had spoken sincerely, seeing her mistake, making this last eager grasp for a happiness. Hope and love glowed in her face and her eyes. Had this happened two months before, Blaise might have taken her away from Conejo.

But . . . Rennie. And now, in this moment, Blaise found that he could not destroy Melanie's dreams. Perhaps later, quietly withdrawing, he could bring her to understand. His face softened and he kissed her, tenderly. She responded so swiftly that Blaise hastily stepped back.

"You'd better get those things put away . . . in case Mark comes back."

"But you and I . . . ?" She left the question expectantly unfinished.

"I — something will work out, somehow."

She took it as answer enough. She replaced the documents and returned them to the high shelf. Blaise walked back to the kitchen, picked up the coffee cup and drank deeply. He wished it had been whisky. When Melanie came out, he stood by the door, hat in hand.

"Leaving so soon?"

"I think — I'd better."

"When will you be back?"

"Soon."

She stepped close, lifted up on her toes and kissed him again. "Very soon, Blaise. I'll wait."

He ducked out the door and walked with swift, long strides to his horse. He swung into saddle and reined the animal around to the gate. Melanie stood in the doorway and she lifted her arm in farewell. Blaise squared around in the saddle and urged the horse to a fast trot. He didn't wave in return.

He turned southward and, a decent distance beyond the house, spurred a fast canter, wanting the feel of the clean air in his face, the sense of action, of distance widening between himself and the Davis house.

His thoughts moved in a giddy whirl. He felt ashamed for himself, and yet justified, too. He recalled the deep surge of sympathy and understanding he had felt for Melanie. For a moment he had seen her impersonally, impassionately, understood what she must feel, and why. In that moment of clarity, the last of his doubts had vanished. He knew that he could never see Rennie in that same, impersonal manner. There would always be an aura about her, the aura of his own feelings and emotions, his own need for her. Not so with Melanie — he no longer loved her.

But Mark? Leonis had said to find the man who bought land, who traded, sold and quietly acquired the Valley acres. Blaise had found that man, now. Blaise understood why, years before, Mark had worked heaven and hell to have them all surrender to Leonis. The King of Calabasas, Mark must have shrewdly realized, could drive rivals off but he could never wholly possess the land. Then the flood and the drought had curtailed Scorpion's expansion. Mark had profited.

But where did Slim Starling's murder fit into the picture? Blaise couldn't fathom that as yet, but he began to understand why Hal had been kidnapped as a warning. Mark feared Blaise, feared he would discover Mark's careful, sly acquisition of acre on acre and, in so doing, uncover the old, old treachery to Paul Case and all the others.

Blaise jerked erect. Mark had suddenly left home just at the time that Vasquez had fled from the hideout, Montanas riders on his heels. As to the old Chavez murder, Blaise saw it in a new light; Mark had coveted Chatsworth land and Chavez had owned a good deal of it.

Mark might logically have placed the incriminating gun and belt in Blaise's shack without suspicion. He could then have sent word to Leonis, who had moved instantly to remove one of his most dangerous opponents. That made sense, though actual proof was lacking. But Starling? Blaise thought he had a hint of a motive in that Slim had come to Simi to start a new wave of settlements in the San Fernando that would strengthen Blaise against Leonis. If Davis feared that his actions in the Valley would be disclosed and that Blaise would remain to hunt for Chavez's killer, then he had a fairly strong motive for shooting Slim.

Blaise gone, Mark would feel safe. Blaise now had no doubt that Mark feared he might lose Melanie, and that in itself would be reason for getting Blaise out of the country.

What of Melanie? She believed Blaise would return for her. Blaise shook his head. Now he need not fear exposing Mark, if he was the real murderer. But Melanie would discover that Blaise could not take Mark's place. She would have lost twice.

Blaise squared his shoulders, sighing. She'd have to be told about Rennie. He would rather work against odds to win Rennie, than to have Melanie for the taking.

"A lot of changes," he said aloud.

. . . and in so short a time.

CHAPTER
NINETEEN

Blaise rode through the pass and drew rein looking down on Calabasas. He could see the whole village, the wide, dusty main street, the road that led out into the Valley beyond. At first glance the town looked as sleepy as ever, but Blaise noted the numerous horses at the hitchracks. Some outfit had ridden into town en masse. Blaise knew it was Scorpion.

He could see the barn behind the grocery store, the guards still at their posts. Men moved in and out of the store; a knot of them stood under the big oak tree. Blaise's lips pressed and he set the horse to the descending road. It was high time the bandits be moved to Los Angeles, a stout jail and long overdue judgment.

An idea struck him and he considered it, looking up to the silent hills, searching each bold crag and dark canyon. He scratched his head, looked down at the town and decided to withhold decision until he knew what had happened in Calabasas.

He entered the town sitting easily in the saddle, eyes sharp and searching. He passed the blacksmith shop, noted the loafers about the open door. They were fresh from the range. They stopped talking and watched him as he rode by. He passed a hitchrack, lined with horses, noted the Scorpion brand. So Leonis had come . . . in strength. The old man planned something, and the old suspicions flared up anew, strong and powerful.

But reason and the knowledge he had acquired in the Conejo intervened. Leonis simply planned direct and fast action, typical of his swift, be-damned way in the past.

"Blaise!"

He drew rein. Hal stepped from the livery stable and waved urgently to him. Blaise kicked the horse into a trot and rode into the yard.

"Leonis rode in. I've been having trouble holding him."

"Why?"

"He wants to stretch a few necks, claims them *bandido* are not worth the long ride to Los Angeles." Hal scratched his head. "He sure hates Vasquez."

Blaise dismounted and loosened the cinch. He grinned crookedly. "Vasquez had laughed at the old man and done as he pleased in these hills. It's pride."

"Maybe, but it sure makes him boil." Hal looked toward the gate. "I told Leonis to keep hands off until you come back. I've half expected Scorpion to rush us."

"Any more men from Montanas?"

"A couple."

"Better get 'em all at the barn. I'll talk to Leonis."

"He's at the saloon, holding powwow with some of his boys."

Blaise nodded and turned the horse over to the hostler, who glared at him and reluctantly accepted the

226

reins. Blaise walked out the gate and across the street to the saloon while Hal hurried away toward the barn.

There were loafers on the saloon porch, Scorpion men. They became still and silent as Blaise walked up, watching him, eyes hostile. Blaise crossed the porch and entered the saloon.

Leonis sat at one of the tables, a few of his riders close about, some of the merchants. As Blaise entered the men turned. Leonis smiled.

"Randell! We've been waiting for you."

"I heard." Blaise walked to the table, looked around at the men and then down at Leonis. "How about a palaver? — Just us?"

Leonis cocked a shaggy brow, considered and then nodded. He glanced at his foreman, the storekeeper. "I'll see you later, boys. The sun's warm on the porch."

The men moved slowly to the door and out. Blaise pulled a chair around. The old man waited calmly, but something in his jaw and eyes showed that he expected antagonism.

"Hal says you're worrying him."

"About those renegades?" Leonis grunted. He folded his hands. "We could hang 'em right here and save time and money."

"You can't do it," Blaise said quietly. Leonis lifted one brow in a high arch.

"Perhaps that we shall see."

Blaise hitched forward. "After ten years in jail on a trumped up charge, I still believe in justice and a fair trial. These men'll get it."

"They're guilty," Leonis said flatly.

"Many a man thought the same of me, I reckon," Blaise snapped. "We'll lock horns over this, Leonis."

The old man sat back, shrewdly watching Blaise. "And what else, Randell? What more you have in mind?"

"Clearing my own name," Blaise said. "Who took over Chavez's land after he was killed?"

"I don't know. I paid no attention to Chatsworth. You could find by the records."

"I'll find them, believe me. I know the man who fits the picture, Leonis. He fits it right down to the ground."

Leonis blinked. "Who!"

Blaise shook his head. "Not yet . . . no real proof. But those bandits out there might bring him into the open. The longer they stay right there, the better chance I got."

"Why?"

"I think my man tied in with Vasquez. He'll be scared these boys might know who he is. Vasquez himself will make a try to get them free, and my man is holding palaver with him right now. Rennie Thatcher's kidnapping broke loose the whole deal. They've got to cover or get out. If I know either of them, they'll not run off without another try."

Leonis stroked his hair and then scratched his chin. "Guessing, I'd say."

"More'n that, Leonis. I know who he is. He knows what's happening here. He'll come." Blaise jerked his thumb over his shoulder to the street. "So I want those renegades held right there."

228

"Until he makes a play . . . or runs out," Leonis nodded. "Afterward?"

"Jail in Los Angeles and a trial."

"A rope and a branch on the oak tree out here."

Blaise sighed. "You'll ride over me to do it, Leonis. But that's to come. Meantime, you and your boys'll let 'em alone?"

"Agreed," Leonis said readily. "But I shall stay here in Calabasas and wait, too. I want to see the end of this."

Blaise arose, grinned. "Fair enough. We'll call a truce for a while. I'll tell Hal."

"I order my men," Leonis agreed. "You fear nothing from Scorpion."

Blaise walked to the store. He told Hal to stop worrying. The Scorpion *segundo* walked from the saloon to the store and gathered the men on the porch around him. They listened and then moved in a body back to the saloon.

"For a drink," Hal said and sighed. "That means Leonis is keeping his bargain. I'll rest tonight."

"I'll stand your turn," Blaise said. "Vasquez may move any time."

"We ain't got enough to hold him off," Hal warned.

"You forget Scorpion's in town. Leonis won't pass up a chance to hit Vasquez. We'll have plenty of guns on our side."

Late that afternoon some Scorpion men rode out but Leonis and the greater number remained in town. They crowded the single café and the saloon, loafed on the store porch or wandered aimlessly up and down the street, played poker in the livery stable. Blaise sent Hal off to bed, while he changed the guards and set himself to an all-night vigil.

The night passed peacefully. Blaise slept most of the day, coming out of the hotel just before sundown to find Scorpion still in the town. Blaise met Leonis in the café and suggested that Scorpion take its share of guarding the bandits.

"Trusting me?" Leonis asked with a slight smile.

"You'd rather have a crack at Vasquez than hang his underdogs. Sure, I trust you . . . that far."

Leonis laughed and gave an order to his *segundo*, who sat across the table. As soon as they finished eating, the *segundo* picked up four of his men and they walked with Blaise to the barn. The Montanas men were surprised, a little suspicious, but glad to be relieved.

Blaise spent another restless night, expecting Vasquez. The bandit would believe that his men were scheduled for a hanging. So would Mark Davis, if he was implicated as Blaise believed. Under the circumstances, they dared not wait too long. Each hour added to the risk.

Yet the night passed and nothing happened. Leonis spoke of it to Blaise the next morning.

"I think perhaps you have guessed wrong. Vasquez was always a coward, a skulker. And perhaps your man is not guilty, after all. We wait one more day. Then we hang 'em."

"We'll see," Blaise said shortly. "I asked you to play it my way."

230

"But how much patience must I have!" Leonis exclaimed.

"You match yours with mine. I'm the one that wins or loses."

Just at sundown a score of riders came in from the east. Blaise stepped out of the hotel porch, stared a moment and then jumped to the street. Thatcher rode at the head of his men and Blaise recognized Rennie's trim figure instantly. They came up to the hotel, Rennie smiling, leaning down and extending her hand to Blaise.

"We couldn't stand it up in the hills. We had to come to see what is happening."

"I'm sure glad to see you," Blaise said, then flushed and looked around at Thatcher. "See you both," he added.

Thatcher smiled and dismounted. A few minutes later in a room upstairs, Blaise recounted what had happened in town, the bargain he had struck with Leonis. Rennie listened, her lips parted. She looked at her father and something passed between them. The old man lit a cigar.

"Then you know who killed Chavez? You have the proof?"

Blaise sighed and sat down on the edge of the bed. "No . . . only I'm certain that's the way things had to happen." He explained the reason for holding the prisoners.

Rennie listened, then looked at her father, who avoided her glance. The girl spoke abruptly with a tone of finality.

"He's right. He has to be. It's good enough for me."

Thatcher frowned deeply and shook his head. "Not good enough yet. Nothing he has will legally clear him . . . that's what counts."

"That counts," Blaise said flatly.

"We'll wait a little longer. If Blaise is right, things will come to a head . . . soon. It's a time to be patient."

He changed the conversation to Leonis, the number of Scorpion men in the town. Half an hour later, Blaise left the hotel. There had been something of double-talk, he sensed, that father and daughter had both spoken with a second meaning that escaped him.

Hal still worried about Scorpion, insisting that Leonis' patience would soon end. "Then we either fight or let those renegades hang," he warned. Blaise calmed Hal's impatience but decided to see for himself how Leonis took the situation.

Night had come again when he found Leonis in the midst of his riders at the saloon. Blaise spent a few moments at the man's table, decided that Hal's fears were baseless. He walked to the crowded bar, had a drink with some Montanas men.

He had just lowered the glass when every man in the room stiffened, listening. The shout sounded closer this time, out on the street.

A man burst through the batwings. "Fire! A big one! Two barns west of town!"

The men poured out the saloon, Blaise among them. A fitful red glow lit the street and Blaise saw flames licking high from two dark buildings. Men raced by, some with buckets. The wind was such that the fire endangered the rest of the town. Leonis saw it, too.

"Git up there!" he roared from the saloon porch. "Want the whole town to go!"

Blaise was jostled as the men hurried by. He held onto a porch support, studying the fire. More men rushed by in the street and Blaise realized that this end of the town would soon be emptied. He jumped off the porch, raced toward the store and the temporary prison behind it.

Just then gunfire broke out, staccato and wicked. Blaise lengthened his stride, jerking his Colt from the holster. He raced the length of the store, the gunfire like thunder, and he could see the spitting flame-tongues from the outer darkness. The guards returned the fire.

Blaise's gun added to the roar. He crouched by the corner of the store throwing slugs with careful precision at the flame lances. Bullets searched him out, and he threw himself flat. He heard slugs hit the store above with a solid thud. One whined high as it glanced off the corner of the rock foundation and made a wicked cut in the air beside Blaise's head.

Dark shapes charged out of the darkness, guns blazing. Blaise fired again and again, and once more had to drop as bullets cut his way. Vasquez had struck, hard and swift, knowing he had little time. He had undoubtedly set the fires at the far end of town as a diversion, depending on a swift attack to release his men.

The guards were outnumbered, but they stood for a while. One of them went down as the renegades swept in. The guards broke and scattered for the protection of the outer darkness, firing as they ran.

The bandits reached the barn, shot off the lock. The doors swung open. Blaise set his teeth, knowing that within seconds Vasquez would win. He fired until his Colt emptied, then hastily ejected shells and crammed new ones into the chambers. The doors swung wider. A bandit dropped, a second grabbed his middle and sank to the earth. But the return fire overwhelmed the guards.

Boots pounded close behind Blaise. A dozen men attacked the barn and Blaise had a fleeting glimpse of Raikes and other Montanas riders. There were shouts down the street that grew louder as Scorpion hurried to join the battle.

Blaise jumped to his feet and joined Montanas. A new burst of fire came from the right as more men converged on the renegades. They milled before the barn and then, realizing they were cut off, they melted inside. The doors closed, and instantly gun flame lanced from the structure as they repelled the charge.

Blaise's shout called the Montanas men back to the store. The attackers to the right faded back, though a steady hail of fire swept the barn. The firing slackened on both sides, a recognition of a temporary stalemate. Blaise moved up to Raikes's side.

"Can you keep that door covered?" he asked.

"A rat couldn't get out," Raikes swore, "without getting shot."

"Where's Thatcher?"

"Somewhere. He sent us helling up here. Just in time."

"I'll find him and Leonis," Blaise said, "to figure out the next move."

"Vasquez holds aces," Raikes said with a motion toward the barn. "We can't get him without losing a hell of a lot of good men."

"He can't get out, either," Blaise said grimly.

He ran to the street. The thoroughfare was deserted. The barns at the far end of town still burned but the flames had died down considerably. A man came rushing up, halted a few feet away, peering into the darkness.

"Blaise?"

"Yes, Hal. Where's Leonis?"

"Holding one side of the barn with the Scorpion boys. They let the townsmen handle the fire."

"Thatcher?"

"Hotel, last I saw him, but bawling for a gun and belt to get in the fracas."

"Vasquez struck like I thought he would," Blaise said, a touch of triumph and worry in his voice. "We've got him trapped, now we have to tie him up."

"A job," Hal said.

"But we'll get him," Blaise snapped. "Let's find Thatcher and Leonis."

He stopped at the hotel. Rennie met him on the steps. She grasped his arms, looked closely at him in the light that streamed from the open door. He had never before seen the true beauty of her face. Her eyes were deep, searching worried . . . afraid for *him*. Her lips were parted and her fingers sank deep into his arms.

They stood looking at one another a long moment and then he held her close and tight, his lips in her hair as she leaned against his chest.

"I was afraid for you," she said. "So afraid, Blaise, so terribly afraid." She drew back and looked searchingly at him, her voice filled with wonder. "What have you done to me? What has happened?"

He smiled and shook his head. "I wondered about it, too, darling. But that's no good. It's enough we're here, us two . . . you and me."

"Yes, it's enough," she answered. Her eyes searched him again. "You're not hurt?"

"Not a scratch. I won't be. Where's Thatcher?"

"He found a gun and left — out there somewhere. He ran toward the saloon."

"I'll find him." He held her closer a moment. "Be careful. Get inside. There might be stray bullets."

"You?" she asked.

"I've got to be out there. Maybe this will clear me. But I can't be hurt now . . . I know it."

He turned and jumped down the steps, hurrying across the street to the saloon. A glance within proved it empty and he walked the length of the porch, dropped to the ground on the far side. Thatcher would be with Leonis. Now and then a gun blasted sporadically. The stalemate continued.

As Blaise turned the corner, he heard the rattle of a wagon in the street and he thought fleetingly it was a hell of a time for anyone to pass through Calabasas.

He found Leonis and Thatcher with the Scorpion men. The barn loomed an uncertain shape in the darkness, lit now and then with orange-red tongues as the renegades fired, more in warning than at actual targets.

"All right," Leonis said when he saw Blaise, "Vasquez come, and he's in that barn. But how do we get him?"

"It looks like an impasse," Thatcher said. "We could wait until daylight, I suppose."

"He'd have the advantage, barricaded inside." Blaise shook his head. "None of us could get near him."

"We could rush the place," Leonis said heavily.

"He's not worth the men we'd lose," Blaise objected.

Hal came up and stood to one side as the three men discussed the problem. He studied the barn, the store, turned and looked toward the street. He elbowed into the circle.

"We can get him. Give me four men."

"How?" Leonis demanded. Hal chuckled. "Come along and see. It's an old Indian trick."

Leonis called four of the nearest men and Hal led the way to the livery stable. He selected an old wagon, loaded it high with hay from the stable loft. Blaise, Leonis and Thatcher watched him for a moment and then Leonis slapped his leg.

"Fire wagon!" He rumbled. "I'll get back to my men so they'll be ready."

Hal paused. "Blaise, you and Thatcher better get our boys ready. It's going to be damned hot for five of us to handle this and Vasquez, too."

Thatcher and Blaise hurried to the store, crouching beside Raikes and telling him to be ready. Soon after Hal and the four Scorpion men came pulling the loaded wagon to the far corner of the store. Hal studied the building, wheeled the wagon around, lashed the tongue to the body so that the wheels would not turn.

"Well, here's for it," he said to Blaise.

"Watch yourself, Hal," Blaise said and moved back to the Montanas men.

A match struck, flamed and died down, and then a small flame licked at the hay. It greedily fanned upward, a dozen flames springing into being and then the whole load burst into fire.

"Let 'er go!" Hal yelled and the five men pushed the wagon directly toward the barn door.

Instantly every outlaw gun blasted at the wagon. It rolled agonizingly slow. Blaise feared that Hal and the others would be cut down before they could cover half the distance. But they were protected by the wagon itself and the vehicle gained momentum. It bowled along the last few yards and crashed into the barn with a thunder that sent the doors sagging, while flames leaped up to the tinder-dry wood of the building.

Leonis and Scorpion closed in. The barn was silent except for the steady mounting sound of the crackling flames. Smoke rolled in thick clouds as Blaise stood poised, tense, waiting. Then it happened.

"There they go!" Blaise yelled. "Hit 'em!"

He lunged forward with Montanas as the renegades jerked the doors back, tearing them from rusty hinges. They came streaming out on either side of the flaming wagon, crouched low, guns blasting.

Instantly Scorpion attacked in a ragged, death-spitting line as Blaise led his men directly toward the barn. The renegades paused uncertainly beyond the wagon, then fanned out, every man for himself. Some ran directly into the Scorpion crew, others toward Blaise and the charging Montanas men. Others raced toward the east to meet with a ragged fire from that direction.

Blaise saw Vasquez. The renegade raced toward him, hatless, Colt held poised, hammer dogged back. At the same instant Vasquez saw him, halted in midstride, and his Colt dropped with a swift, chopping motion. Blaise flung himself to one side, firing from the hip. Vasquez' bullet whipped by him, but Blaise's bullet staggered the outlaw. Only for a second. The man wheeled with the speed of a striking snake, sending another shot at Blaise that cut so close Blaise fell sprawling. In another second the outlaw had vanished beyond the reach of the flames. Blaise scrambled to his feet and raced after him.

He wanted Vasquez, wanted him alive and able to talk. He broke through the ring of townsmen and cowboys, catching no glimpse of Vasquez. Gun thunder still roared, but Blaise caught a slight move in the shadows ahead and he raced toward it, gun held ready.

But he found nothing. He pushed on, moving this way and that, searching, alert. The gunfire slackened and then ceased altogether. The fighting was over, but there was still Vasquez somewhere just ahead. He was wounded, but Blaise didn't know how badly. He had to be found.

Blaise searched far beyond the eastern edge of the town. At last he stopped, knowing that he had no chance in this blind hunt of a whole valley and a range of mountains. Vasquez, at least, had escaped. After this defeat he would not come back to Calabasas. He was gone and, with him, the chance for Blaise to clear himself.

Blaise wearily shoved his gun in the holster, turned and walked despondently back toward the town. Now and then a gun blasted, but the sound was intermittent, beyond the town, where the last of the fleeing renegades were hunted down. Blaise thought dispiritedly that after this night, Calabasas would settle into peaceful ways. It would no longer be the wild and woolly town of legend at the far end of the Valley.

It was high time. This land was made for peace. Even if ranching was such that only a few could run cattle, there would be farms and more towns out where the vacant Valley land stretched, perhaps even cities if a man would let his dreams go beyond reasonable bounds.

He passed the first house of the village, plodding now, weary and discouraged. He might play a part in the future of this land but there would always be that stigma against him. Whoever killed Chavez would never be revealed. If it was Mark Davis, he had only to do nothing and the murder trail was lost. Vasquez was gone beyond recall, out into the dark stretches of the night. The game had been played . . . and Blaise had lost.

A gun blasted just behind him with a jarring thunder that jerked Blaise half around as the bullet whipped close. He completed the spin and dropped as though the slug had found its mark. He jerked his Colt free as he fell sprawling and lay inert.

His ears strained into the night and he searched the shadows without moving his head. There was no sound beyond the deep growl of the crowd in the distant street, an occasional faint shout. Then a shadow moved not far away.

Blaise tensed and waited, thumb inching up to the hammer spur.

Perhaps he had not lost altogether, after all.

CHAPTER
TWENTY

There was no more movement for long tense moments, then a step sounded, slow, cautious, testing, brush moved with a faint whisper. Blaise's fingers tightened on the gun grip. The step sounded louder, closer. Blaise tried to judge the distance between him and the man who moved so carefully.

Then Hal King shouted near by. The shadow froze. Hal came blundering on, called again. Blaise slowly brought up his feet, ready to spring.

The shadow whirled, slammed a shot at Hal, and raced away toward the buildings that lined the south side of the near-by street. Blaise scrambled to his feet, lifted his gun. A Colt blasted and the bullet sped close. Hal had mistaken Blaise for the ambusher and had fired blindly into the darkness.

Blaise flinched, yelled Hal's name and raced after the fleeing shadow. He could hear the man ahead, the pound of boots behind him. Hal fired again, the bullet whining off to the left, but obviously aimed at Blaise.

A flame blossomed ahead, a swift, explosive mushroom of color that instantly snuffed out. The slug whined by and then the man raced on. Blaise snapped a shot. He dared not wait for Hal or he would lose the man ahead.

They passed the glowing embers of the prison several yards to their right. The man headed for a line of outbuildings not far ahead. They reached the sheds. Blaise had his first, fleeting glimpse of the man as he turned a corner into light and disappeared.

Blaise reached the corner, just as Hal fired a fusillade that sounded like rolling thunder in the night. From somewhere out on the street, men shouted alarm. Blaise thought grimly that they would trap the fleeing man in a matter of minutes. He raced on.

A figure was silhouetted momentarily against the light from the street. Evidently he realized that only one man was close but that others closed in. He whirled about and the gun spoke again.

The bullet caught Blaise on the collar bone with the force of a sledge hammer. He hit the ground, rolled over, twisted toward the gunman. The man still stood, tense, poised. Blaise lifted his gun and fired. The man jerked. Blaise caught the glitter of his weapon as he raised it. Then he turned and faded into the shadows as nausea gripped Blaise and the world started spinning.

He fought to keep above the black tide that rose to engulf him. He pulled himself up, felt the dull throb of his shoulder, the strange feeling that the bone had melted and the flesh was empty. Hal came pounding up, halted a yard or so away, and then darted forward. He leaned down, gun ready.

"Blaise! For God's sake, was it you ahead of me all the time!"

"Me . . . and someone else," Blaise gritted. Hal looked up and around, but Blaise shook his head. "He's gone. I winged him, but he got away."

"I — shot you?" Hal demanded.

"No. We'd better look at this shoulder of mine."

Hal helped him to his feet. Blaise stood swaying a moment, gripping his shoulder, then lifted his left arm and cradling it as he walked to the street, Hal close beside him, worried and chagrined.

The street was filled with Scorpion and Montanas riders, men and women of the town, wide eyed with excitement and the swift pace of events. They parted to let Blaise and Hal through, and finally they entered the hotel.

Blaise stopped short just inside the door. Paul, Walt and Melanie turned to face him. Melanie searched his face, then her eyes dropped to his bloodstained shoulder, the injured arm.

"Blaise!" She rushed to him, all solicitation. She helped him to a chair and he sat down, grateful. "You're hurt! Get a doctor!"

"Here, Mel." Paul pushed her aside. "I'll see what it is."

He unbuttoned Blaise's shirt and gingerly pulled it back from the wound. Blaise felt nausea grip him, and he gritted his teeth against it, asked a question as an anodyne.

"When did you get here?"

Paul pulled the shirt back further, pursed his lips as he studied the wound. "Just when things were breaking wide open. Mel told me and Mark about Vasquez and that you had some of his men here. We thought you might need help, what with him and Leonis. Mel said she was coming and, for once, we couldn't leave her at home."

"Mark wanted to come?"

Paul carefully ripped the shirt away so that there was no pull or pressure on the shoulder. "You may have a smashed bone, Blaise. First thing is to stop the bleeding." He bent down to the wound again. "Yes, Mark insisted on coming. Surprised me a little, but I figured you could use every man."

"Where is he?"

"He went out to find you, to see how he could help," Mel said hurriedly. She stroked her hand along his brow. "He'll — be all right, Dad?"

"Sure. Maybe a stiff shoulder, but nothing serious once he stops bleeding like a stuck pig."

Blaise felt Melanie's hand halt abruptly and it seemed as if the fingers taloned. He looked up to see her staring across the room toward the stairs. Rennie stood there, poised, one hand tight on the stair-rail, her face white and strained. She came across the room, pushed Paul aside.

"Blaise!"

He smiled. "It's all right . . . a busted shoulder that'll mend."

Rennie looked around at Paul, a question in her eyes. He nodded, looked curiously at Blaise. Melanie's hand fell away and she stepped back. Blaise introduced Rennie to Paul and then to Melanie. Mel murmured something, looked at Blaise, back to Rennie again.

She half lifted her hand, then let her arm fall heavily. Something left her face and her lips quivered slightly. She stepped further back as Rennie gave her full attention to Blaise. She helped Paul bandage the wound and make a sling for the arm. Melanie watched, despair in her eyes.

Blaise winced at a pressure of Paul's fingers and lifted his head. The pain passed and he became aware of Melanie, the stricken question that her eyes asked. He looked at her, forgetting the rest, knowing that she now understood. He felt the force of the unspoken question and something in his own face must have given her the answer. She breathed deeply, slowly exhaled with a long sigh and turned away.

Blaise turned to face the door just as Mark walked in. Their eyes met, locked. Mark stopped short. He wore a coat, unbuttoned so that the heavy buckle of his gun belt showed. The edge of the holster showed beneath it. His face was tight, the lips pressed firmly beneath the mustache. He nodded faintly and turned to go out again. Just then Paul Case looked over his shoulder.

"Mark!" he called, "Blaise has been wounded."

Mark turned again, slowly. "Bad?" he asked in a strained voice.

"Broken collar bone, I think. See if you can find the doctor."

"Sure," he said in the same tight voice, "Sure . . . right away."

"Mark!" Melanie said it sharply and Mark half turned again.

Blaise followed Melanie's stricken look to the floor just at Mark's feet. A dark blob appeared, faded into the carpet. Then another. Blaise's eyes lifted upward to the man's coat sleeve just as another drop of blood formed from between his fingers.

Hal made a strangled sound and his Colt jumped from the holster, dropped to line on the man in the doorway. Mark stood immobile, his face paling. Then he saw the blood. His head jerked up, like a cornered animal, but Hal's leveled gun held him motionless.

The others stood frozen and silent as Hal moved across the room. He jerked back Mark's coat, lifted the gun from the holster. He passed the muzzle under his nose and then looked down into the cylinders.

"One shell left, and it smells of powder." He looked up. "What about it?"

Mark stood very quiet, his gaze shifted to the others, one by one, reading their faces, their eyes. Without warning he whirled and lunged to the door, before Hal could lift his weapon.

Just then Leonis stepped in. Mark struck the big man head on and both staggered back, Mark losing his balance and falling. Instantly Hal stepped over him. Mark froze, staring into the black gun muzzle. Hal stepped back a pace, remaining between Mark and the door.

"Get up," he ordered. "Take off that coat."

Mark remained crouched, then he pulled himself up, using only one arm. The other hung limp. He stared at Hal and then shot a swift glance at the others. He licked his lips and his face grew paper white. Blood dropped more regularly to the floor. Mark half lifted his hand to the top coat-button. Then cold sweat broke out on his face and he collapsed.

Paul jumped to his side and Melanie was close beside him. She bent down and then slowly straightened without touching her husband. She looked at Hal.

"How — did you know he was — ?"

"Blaise and me had a brush with a bushwhacker. He nearly got Blaise and he threw some slugs at me. Neither of us had a good look, but Blaise winged the gent. I saw blood drip from his hand. There was only one way he could've been winged."

"He's coming around," Paul said.

Blaise pulled himself from the chair and pushed through to Paul's side, crouching down as Mark opened his eyes and looked up at him. Fear showed plainly.

"So you wanted me dead, Mark," Blaise said quietly. "Why?"

Mark stared at him, tried to sit up, but fell back. "Bad?" he asked.

"You've got it real bad, Mark," Blaise said swiftly. "You only got a little time to talk."

Paul reached toward the man's coat, but Blaise's hand checked him, and he made a swift negative gesture. "Just a little time, Mark . . . and I know most of it."

"What do you know?" Mark asked in a whisper that still retained a faint, ragged note of defiance.

"You're the one who bought up tax lands and homesteads, Mark, including a part of my own ranch. You're the one who hired Vasquez to kidnap Hal and warn him and me out of the country . . . or kill us if we didn't run." Blaise took a long chance. "We've got that from the prisoners, because Vasquez boasted how smart he was. You wanted me out of the country or dead, Mark, because you were afraid."

Mark's lips twisted. He closed his eyes and sighed wearily. He spoke in a hoarse whisper, eyes still closed. "You want my wife, Randell!" His eyes snapped open and desperation showed in them. "Damn you, don't let me lay here and die! Get a doctor!"

Melanie stiffened and clapped her hand over her mouth, face pale and eyes wide. Paul inched forward but Blaise checked him again.

"Why, Mark? I told you it was bad. You tried another murder. You lost."

Mark stared at him. "Another . . . you . . . know?"

"Chavez and Starling? You might as well tell it all, Mark — while you've still got breath."

He had lost blood and it made him weak, but Blaise shrewdly estimated he had not as yet reached the danger point. Now the shoulder wound began to pain and Mark's lips twisted. Fear placed sweat drops on his forehead. He remained silent and defiant a moment longer and then it all left him with a rush. He was sure he was dying and stark fear sank talons into his mind. His head dropped back and he spoke in a dead, flat tone as though nothing mattered any more.

"I knew you'd dig up that old Chavez killing and finally pin it on me. I knew it. I had to stop you. He was a drunken, stubborn, damn' Mexican who drew a knife on me when I tried to talk business. I shot him."

"But not then, Mark," Blaise insisted. Mark licked his lips.

"No, not then. I ran. But I waited for him and got him. You kept wanting to fight Leonis and I saw a way to get rid of you."

"You planted the gun and holster and then sent word to Leonis, Mark. Why?"

"If Paul and the others gave up their land, Leonis could only take part of it. He wouldn't know when I bought up homestead claims and paid up the back taxes."

"So now you own most of the west Valley, Mark?"

"Most?" A touch of pride came in Mark's voice and he opened his eyes. "I own all but a few acres here and there."

"And Starling?"

"I met him outside Simi and he told me what you and him planned to do. You'd go back in there and file claims and then you'd learn what I'd done. He was going to help you find out what really happened to Chavez, he said. It rattled me and I — shot him without thinking."

Blaise shook his head. "Murder, Mark, and you tried to get me. But land wasn't all the reason."

"Melanie," Mark half whispered. "You were safe in jail forever and then luck got you out. The first day at the farm I saw the way you looked at her . . .

250

hungry-like. You're in love with her, Randell, and you'd take her from me. She's mine, damn you!"

Blaise slowly stood up. He looked at Paul and Leonis and then to Hal, the men nodding. Then he looked at Melanie who stared down in pale horror at her husband. Rennie watched Blaise in a questioning, searching way. Blaise sighed and rubbed his hand along his levis as though to clean it.

"Patch him up, Paul. He ain't lost much blood. Leonis, we can take him in with the rest to Los Angeles?"

"Glad to get his kind out of Calabasas!" the big man growled. Mark stared at Blaise, puzzled.

"You mean — ?"

"You're a long way from dying," Blaise finished. "It's another mistake you made, Mark. You were mistaken about Melanie and me. You made just one right guess. I sure meant to trace Chavez's killer down if it took the rest of my life."

He looked up at the men. "You'll be witness to what he said?"

"Sure!" Leonis snapped. Paul and Hal only nodded. Suddenly Mark sat up and tried to scramble to his feet.

"Damn you! Oh, damn —"

He fell backward in another faint. Paul distastefully ripped back the coat to stop the blood and bandage the wound. Melanie stood stricken. Blaise started to say something to her and realized its futility.

He caught Hal's soft gaze as he looked at the girl, his heart in his eyes. Blaise blinked and remembered that Hal had looked at her this way before. But now there was a touch of hope that she was not far off and unobtainable. If Mel had never really loved Mark, then she would recover from this blow. Melanie sank back into a chair and covered her face with her hands.

Blaise turned and walked out on the porch. The crowd still milled in the street, but at the dark, far end of the porch there was obscurity and comparative peace. He thoughtfully rolled a cigarette. Everything had so depended on the slender thread of Mark's fear and belief in death that Blaise even now shuddered at the narrow margin by which he had finally won.

Someone stirred near by and Blaise turned. Rennie stood a few feet away. Lamplight from the window caught the soft line of her cheek and jaw, the sober lips. Just then Thatcher appeared from the crowd and started to climb the steps.

"Father," Rennie called. "Blaise and I are over here."

Thatcher checked and came up to them.

"Three more prisoners than we had to begin with," he said with satisfaction. "We'll see no more of that renegade, Vasquez."

"A fourth prisoner, Father," Rennie said. "Inside, Blaise just cleared his name."

"What!"

Rennie told him of what had happened and Thatcher swore softly in amazement. Then he took Blaise's hand. "I'm glad, son."

"Father . . . now?" Rennie asked. Thatcher looked at her, then up at Blaise. He chuckled.

"Now."

She came up to Blaise and placed her hands on his shoulders, eyes intent upon him. "Do you love me, Blaise?"

His mouth dropped open and the cigarette fell from his fingers. He tried to speak but his lips only fumbled the words, no sound came forth. Thatcher chuckled again.

"Answer her, Blaise. Do you?"

"I . . . why . . ." But his answer was enough. Thatcher placed his hand on Rennie's arm, and one on Blaise's shoulder.

"You've done more'n any other young man, Blaise. Rennie loves you. But I insisted that she wait until you had completely cleared yourself of murder. You've done it, son. I'm damned proud of you."

"But —"

"Now wait, son. You're the kind of man I've always wanted to see come along. Quit fidgeting, Rennie! I'll say my piece and leave you.

"You'll be manager of Las Montanas, son, and someday its owner, along with my daughter. I'll be going back east in a few months, be gone maybe a year. But I'll leave my ranch and my daughter in good hands. Now, boy, count five after I'm gone and ask her to marry you."

He clapped Blaise on the shoulder, kissed his daughter and strode jauntily into the hotel. Blaise faced the girl, the lovely girl with violet eyes whom he had met by chance on the stage, the girl whose reality had replaced a lost dream, who had herself become a dream and a far-distant goal. She stood here and now, close . . . and his.

She tapped her foot, a slight impatient sound. But her lips smiled.

"When in the world," she asked in a whisper, "will I ever be kissed?"

He answered.

ISIS publish a wide range of books in large print, from fiction to biography. Any suggestions for books you would like to see in large print or audio are always welcome. Please send to the Editorial Department at:

ISIS Publishing Limited
7 Centremead
Osney Mead
Oxford OX2 0ES

A full list of titles is available free of charge from:

Ulverscroft Large Print Books Limited

(UK)
The Green
Bradgate Road, Anstey
Leicester LE7 7FU
Tel: (0116) 236 4325

(Australia)
P.O. Box 314
St Leonards
NSW 1590
Tel: (02) 9436 2622

(USA)
P.O. Box 1230
West Seneca
N.Y. 14224-1230
Tel: (716) 674 4270

(Canada)
P.O. Box 80038
Burlington
Ontario L7L 6B1
Tel: (905) 637 8734

(New Zealand)
P.O. Box 456
Feilding
Tel: (06) 323 6828

Details of **ISIS** complete and unabridged audio books are also available from these offices. Alternatively, contact your local library for details of their collection of **ISIS** large print and unabridged audio books.